# Mark of the Baskerville Hound

## Wilfred J. "Chick" Huettel

Paperback ISBN 978-1-78092-088-7
ePub ISBN 978-1-78092-089-4
PDF ISBN 978-1-78092-090-0

Published in the UK by MX Publishing
335 Princess Park Manor, Royal Drive, London, N11 3GX
www.mxpublishing.com

Cover artwork by www.staunch.com

# Dedication

To my classical wife, Cathy, and my lovely daughters, Julie and Missy, who always gave me encouragement. Also Wendy Anderson, my most precious critic and advisor.

# Introduction

This small introduction is dedicated to Chief. In the 1939 classic film *The Hound of the Baskervilles*, starring Basil Rathbone, Nigel Bruce, and Richard Greene, there was another great actor. Embellished with foam, sparkle, black shoe polish, and a florescent substance, Chief was a trained, 140-pound Great Dane that made the movie hauntingly beautiful. "Blitzen" was his real name, but the movie publicity department said it sounded too German. Thus Blitzen was given a stage name...Chief. The movie's producer, Gene Markey, said of Chief, "A friendly old Great Dane, who despite all his yelping, cannot make his bark worse than his bite." Not much is known of his further acting accomplishments. He now rests somewhere in the San Fernando Valley, California.

----------- ----------- -----------

For those who have never read the immortal mystery of Sir Arthur Conan Doyle's classic *The Hound of the Baskervilles* or seen some of the various movie versions, I shall attempt to give a short synopsis of the events. However, to understand the full impact of *Mark of the Baskerville Hound*, it simply cannot be overstated that the reader must take time to sit back in a soft lounge chair on a rainy, wind-driven night before a crackling fireplace and delve into Doyle's marvelous story published in 1901. Of all the dark gothic mystery novels that followed after Sir Arthur Conan Doyle's Dartmoor saga, there has simply been no equal to his. The original sets the stage for *Mark of the Baskerville Hound*. So let us begin with a summary of the events in *The Hound of the Baskervilles*.

5

A Dr. James Mortimer contacts Mr. Sherlock Holmes, along with Holmes' cohort, Dr. John Watson, of 221-B Baker Street, London, and reveals his fear of the Baskerville curse—a curse said to have killed many of the hereditary owners of Baskerville Hall, which is located in the desolate moor area of Dartmoor, England. The recent death of the elderly Sir Charles Baskerville, who was found with large dog footprints around his body, has only confirmed the legend. From an old and crackled parchment Dr. Mortimer reads to Holmes and Watson the legend that was written by one of the early Baskerville ancestors. It was dated 1742.

----------- ----------- -----------

## The Legend

"Of the origin of the Hound of the Baskervilles there have been many statements, yet as I come in a direct line from Hugo Baskerville, and as I had the story from my father, who also had it from his, I have set it down with all belief that it occurred even as is here set forth. And I would have you believe, my sons, that the same Justice which punishes sin may also most graciously forgive it, and that no ban is so heavy but that by prayer and repentance it may be removed. Learn then from this story not to fear the fruits of the past, but rather to be circumspect in the future, that those foul passions whereby our family has suffered so grievously may not again be loosed to our undoing.

"Know then that in the time of the Great Rebellion (the history of which by the learned Lord Clarendon I most earnestly commend to your attention) this Manor of Baskerville was held by Hugo of that name, nor can it be gainsaid that he was a most wild, profane, and godless man. This, in truth, his neighbors might have pardoned, seeing that saints have never flourished in those parts, but there was in him a certain wanton and cruel humour which made his name a byword through the West. It chanced that this Hugo came to love (if, indeed, so dark a passion may be known under so bright a name) the daughter of a yeoman who held lands near the Baskerville estate. But the young maiden, being discreet and of good repute, would ever avoid him, for she feared his evil name. So it came to pass that one Michaelmas this Hugo, with five or six of his idle and wicked companions, stole down upon the farm and carried off the maiden, her father and brothers being from home, as he well knew. When they had brought her to the Hall the maiden was placed in an upper chamber, while Hugo and his friends sat down to a long carouse, as was their nightly custom. Now, the poor lass upstairs was like to have her wits turned at the singing and shouting and terrible oaths which came up to her from below, for they say that the words used by Hugo Baskerville, when he was in wine, were such as might blast the man who said them. At last in the stress of her fear she did that which might have daunted the bravest or most active man, for by the aid of the growth of ivy which covered (and still covers) the south wall she came down from under the eaves, and so homeward across the moor, there being three leagues betwixt the Hall and her father's farm.

"It chanced that some little time later Hugo

left his guests to carry food and drink—with other worse things, perchance—to his captive, and so found the cage empty and the bird escaped. Then, as it would seem, he became as one that hath a devil, for, rushing down the stairs into the dining-hall, he sprang upon the great table, flagons and trenchers flying before him, and he cried aloud before all the company that he would that very night render his body and soul to the Powers of Evil if he might but overtake the wench. And while the revellers stood aghast at the fury of the man, one more wicked or, it may be, more drunken than the rest, cried out that they should put the hounds upon her. Whereat Hugo ran from the house, crying to his grooms that they should saddle his mare and unkennel the pack, and giving the hounds a kerchief of the maid's, he swung them to the line, and so off full cry in the moonlight over the moor.

"Now, for some space the revellers stood agape, unable to understand all that had been done in such haste. But anon their bemused wits awoke to the nature of the deed which was like to be done upon the moorlands. Everything was now in an uproar, some calling for their pistols, some for their horses, and some for another flask of wine. But at length some sense came back to their crazed minds, and the whole of them, thirteen in number, took horse and started in pursuit. The moon shone clear above them, and they road swiftly abreast, taking that course which the maiden must needs have taken if she were to reach her own home.

"They had gone a mile or two when they

passed one of the night shepherds upon the moorlands, and they cried to him to know if he had seen the hunt. And the man, as the story goes, was so crazed with fear that he could scarce speak, but at last he said that he had indeed seen the unhappy maiden, with the hounds upon her track. 'But I have seen more than that,' said he, 'for Hugo Baskerville passed me upon his black mare, and there ran mute behind him such a hound of hell as God forbid should ever be at my heels.' So the drunken squires cursed the shepherd and rode onward. But soon their skins turned cold, for there came a galloping across the moor, and the black mare, dabbled with white froth, went past with trailing bridle and empty saddle. Then the revellers rode close together, for a great fear was on them, but they still followed over the moor, though each, had he been alone, would have been right glad to have turned his horse's head. Riding slowly in this fashion they came at last upon the hounds. These, though known for their valour and breed, were whimpering in a cluster at the head of a deep dip or goyal, as we call it, upon the moor, some slinking away and some, with starting hackles and staring eyes, gazing down the narrow valley before them.

"The company had come to a halt, more sober men, as you may guess, than when they started. The most of them would by no means advance, but three of them, the boldest, or it may be the most drunken, rode forward down the goyal. Now, it opened into a broad space in which stood two of those great stones, still to be seen there, which were set by certain forgotten peoples in days of old. The moon was shining bright upon the clearing, and there in the centre lay the unhappy maid where she had fallen, dead of fear and of fatigue. But it was not the sight of her body, nor yet was it that of the body of Hugo Baskerville lying near her, which raised the hair upon the heads of these three daredevil roysterers, but it was that, standing over Hugo, and plucking at his throat, there stood a foul thing, a great, black beast, shaped like a hound, yet larger than any hound that ever mortal eye has rested upon. And even as they looked the thing tore the throat out of Hugo Baskerville, on which, as it turned its blazing eyes and dripping jaws upon them, the three shrieked with fear and rode for dear life, still screaming, across the moor. One, it is said, died that very night of what he had seen, and the other twain were but broken men for the rest of their days.

"Such is the tale, my sons, of the coming of the hound which is said to have plagued the family so sorely ever since. If I have set it down it is because that which is clearly known hath less terror than that which is but hinted at and guessed. Nor can it be denied that many of the family have been unhappy in their deaths, which have been sudden, bloody, and mysterious. Yet may we shelter ourselves in the infinite goodness of Providence, which would not forever punish the innocent beyond that third or fourth generation which is threatened in Holy Writ. To that Providence, my sons, I hereby commend you, and I counsel you by way of caution to forbear from crossing the moor in those dark hours when the powers of evil are exalted."

----------- ----------- -----------

When the new inheritor, Sir Henry Baskerville, arrives in London from Canada, Dr. Mortimer entrusts the young Henry to the protection of Mr. Holmes. Quickly events begin to happen. The young Baskerville is threatened with a note to not go to Baskerville Hall, plus one of his boots is stolen from his hotel room. Nevertheless, Henry is determined that he is not to be denied his inheritance. Unable to accompany the new owner of the Baskerville estate and Dr. Mortimer back to Dartmoor because of impending matters, Holmes sends Dr. Watson to guard the young heir and report any unusual circumstances.

During the visit Dr. Watson reports to Holmes by letter about the various neighbors surrounding the estate and the foreboding atmosphere of Dartmoor. There he and Sir Henry discover the Baskerville Hall butler, Barrymore, sending signals by candle to another distant light on the moor. It turns out the other light belongs to Selden, a half-crazed murderer who had escaped from the local prison.

While Watson is walking on the moor, he meets a man named Stapleton who is a naturalist. Stapleton shows the doctor the various sights and dangers on the moor, which are mainly slushy bogs that can suck a man under if he should happen to fall into the trap. They see a wild moor pony stuck and it disappears under the mud. Then they hear a howling in the far distance. Watson also meets Stapleton's sister, who, thinking Watson is Henry Baskerville, secretly warms him to return to London.

Later, as Watson relates to Holmes, Sir Henry meets Miss Stapleton and shows signs of a budding romantic air for her. She again tries to warn Sir Henry to leave the area, but Stapleton intervenes, accusing Sir Henry of improper advances toward his sister. Stapleton later apologizes for his outburst and invites Sir Henry to dine at his home.

One day Watson and Henry confront Barrymore and his wife, confess that they have been helping the convict because he is her brother. Together Watson and Sir Henry attempt to capture Selden one evening, but the murderer escapes them in the darkness, followed by the sound of a howling hound.

As they head back to the manor, in the distance Dr. Watson spots a thin man silhouetted against the moon observing them. Barrymore tells Watson that the convict Selden told him that a stranger has been hiding in some stone ruins out on the moor and that a young boy brings him food at various times. A neighbor spots the boy through a telescope and informs Watson that the child is helping the escaped murderer.

A twist in the case comes when a woman in the village confesses that she wrote a note to old Sir Charles Baskerville asking for financial help and that he arranged to meet her in the manor garden the night he was found dead. She later found other means of assistance, not suspecting that her benefactor was actually the villain.

Next Watson begins the hunt for the stranger on the moor. The doctor locates the hideout and waits inside with his pistol at the ready. When a man comes near the shelter, Watson calls out—and suddenly he is confronted by Holmes who had been camping in the ruins.

Dr. Watson is upset that he was not informed of Holmes' plan to spy about the moor. Holmes calms Watson and informs him that Stapleton is the villain and that his sister, Miss Stapleton, is really his wife. Yet Holmes does not yet understand what exactly Stapleton is up to or why he wants the Baskervilles dead. And to complicate matters, Holmes has learned that Stapleton is having an affair with the woman in the village who wrote to Sir Charles to meet her the night that the dog chased the Baskerville owner to death.

Holmes goes on to explain to Watson that through investigation he has discovered that Stapleton's wife was the one who sent Sir Henry the note in London because she was desperately trying to warn him to be careful.

Suddenly Holmes and Watson hear a man's cry for help along with a howl. By the time they reach the man, he has fallen to his death at the base of a cliff, and they recognize him as the convict Selden. The dead convict is dressed in Sir Henry's old clothes, which the Baskerville butler had given him out of charity so he could stay warm out on the moor. Suddenly, Stapleton appears and says he happened to be in the area and heard the commotion. Holmes sees that Stapleton is surprised that the clothed man was not Sir Henry. Stapleton takes his leave as Holmes ponders that both dead men (Sir Charles Baskerville and Selden the convict) had been killed by running to their deaths and neither victim had bite marks on his body.

One evening when Holmes is at the manor with Watson, he notices an old oil portrait among the various paintings of past lords of the manor. There he is surprised to see a likeness of Stapleton. He informs Watson that they now have a motive and Sir Henry is, indeed, in very great danger. Stapleton is after the inheritance of a long-lost ancestor—he too is descended from the Baskervilles. Holmes and Watson keep this knowledge to themselves for the time being.

Making up an excuse for business in London, Holmes informs Sir Henry that he and Watson must return on the train. With the threat of the convict Selden gone, Holmes encourages Sir Henry to keep his dinner appointment with Stapleton and assures him that he and Watson shall return shortly. Holmes also asks Sir Henry to take his carriage that evening to Stapleton's house and walk back.

Bringing back Inspector Lestrade of Scotland Yard from London, Holmes meets the woman from the village and informs her he knows all. He tells her that he knows that Stapleton encouraged her to write the letter that brought Sir Charles out into the garden. Then Stapleton released a giant hound to terrify Sir Charles, whom he knew was afraid of the curse. This caused the death of the heart-troubled, old knight of Baskerville.

Hiding in the brush, Holmes and Watson spy Stapleton dining alone in his home with Sir Henry. Mrs. Stapleton is nowhere to be seen. Then a deep fog rolls in. Next they see Sir Henry running and behind him a huge black hound. The glowing hound pounces on Sir Henry while Watson and Holmes shoot at the dog. After being hit by five bullets, the dog rolls over dead. Florescent phosphorus rubbed on the poor, starved creature reveals what gave it the hellish appearance. They then hunt for Mrs. Stapleton and find her beaten and locked in a room. She tells them she thinks her husband has escaped through the moor and is headed toward the Grimpen Mire.

The next day the group, along with Mrs. Stapleton, heads toward the Grimpen Mire. They find the young Sir Henry's old boot that Stapleton had stolen and used to entice the hungry hound to follow Sir Henry's scent. The reason the dog had chased Selden the convict was because he was wearing Henry's clothes. After becoming stuck in the cold bog, the group heads back without ever finding Stapleton.

A few weeks later Dr. Mortimer and Sir Henry visit 221-B Baker Street. They have learned that Stapleton came all the way from South America to claim the inheritance. But the elderly Sir Charles and the young Henry were obstacles in his way. Stapleton originally wanted to kill young Henry in London, but his plan was thwarted. Stapleton's wife refused to be a part of the crime, so Stapleton then enticed the village woman to help him with promises of her becoming his wife. Both women had been threatened and duped by Stapleton's devious planning.

Holmes explains that he had made the decision to become a

moor phantom so that his notoriety would not hinder the investigation. He used Dr. Watson to lay the groundwork. With Stapleton's plan thwarted and the dog dead, thus the "Hound" legend ended…

Or did it?

## Mark of the Baskerville Hound

This is the story of a rational man and an irrational experience. Or perhaps it's a man's irrational mind attempting to cope with a rational event. Either way, it's for you to judge.

# Chapter 1

Mid-August 1982. New York City. A man in his T-shirt and shorts stared out of his fourth-floor apartment window. The casement air conditioner was having a hard time keeping the small apartment cool in the intense nighttime humidity. He recently had it repaired, but the top rooms were predictably uncomfortable in the summer. About the only relief was the music coming in lyrical waves from two small speakers located on a cluttered bookshelf that covered the entire living room wall. The shelves then turned a corner with more mismatched books and even invaded the small dining room. The melody was his favorite aria, "Ruhe sanft mein holder leben," from Mozart's uncompleted opera *Zaide*. Somehow the notes escaped through the windows and just barely echoed throughout the apartment courtyard. More books and sheets of notebook paper were strewn on the coffee table and the couch, and nearly every other table had an assortment of yellow or white typed paper. An unemptied silver ashtray spilling over with filter cigarette butts sat on top of a small television. The only space for the TV was on a desk pushed up to a corner in the entrance to the cubical type kitchen. Each of the apartment complex windows looked across from one another and diagonally as well. As a matter of fact, the whole layout constantly reminded him of the Alfred Hitchcock film *The Rear Window*.

As it was around midnight or so, most of the picture glass windows were dark, and those still lit were hidden by blinds. Only a small lamp in the man's bedroom glowed. The ever-present wailing of an emergency siren came from somewhere on the streets. Since he had returned from England those dark streets were no longer safe—too many red lights. The color of any red glimmer immediately instilled a shaking fear in him. But lately he felt uneasy even during daylight hours. He had the constant feeling he was being stalked.

He looked into the bedroom at the unmade bed. He remembered that in high school he was required to read *Moby Dick*. What was it that Captain Ahab said about his cabin berth? Oh yeah, it was his coffin with a shroud, or something like that. His bed was like that, and he understood Ahab's despairing remark. He put his drink down, lay down in the tangled bed sheets, and snapped out the light. A bolt-of-lightning pain struck his right knee. A bullet wound had brought about his early retirement a few years past, and he never knew when the wound would surprise him with a mean reminder of the drug bust that led to a full-fledged shootout. He rubbed it for a few minutes. Then it went away as quick as it came. Slowly, a fog with white wisps of swirling tentacles wrapped around him. Then a ruby-colored radiance emerged as if penetrating through his closed eyelids. And lastly, the always-familiar sounds of hoofs beating the ground began to pound his ears. Then it all vanished as he sank into the abyss.

At exactly 3:15 A.M. it happened. The man's screams shattered the silence.

The unnerving wail was heard through every tenant wall, and it reverberated back and forth in the complex's community courtyard. He sat straight up, his pillow was wet, and perspiration droplets glistened on his face in a haphazard fashion. He had the shakes again—just when he thought it might be over. Lights flickered on about the building, and the yells and wall-pounding that signaled annoyance began. An unhappy baby joined in the chorus. Then came the expected banging on his door.

"You nut case! This is Rico. If you do that one more time I'm a gonna bust this door in and smack you so hard you'll never

19

wake up! You're a mental freak. You need to be locked up!"

One of the aroused apartment window lights cast a sliver of light through his bent bedroom window blind and targeted only his eyes. They were puffy and red, worn and yellow, each one sitting in their deep, gray and black sockets. They were the eyes of an exhausted man. The next moment, as the stream of light changed and highlighted his glazed pupils, a tear slipped out and down to his upper lip.

----------- ----------- -----------

Old St. Anne's Catholic Church was just that—worn out and almost beyond restoration. Nothing worked properly save the front door lock. The air conditioning was out temporarily, but the thick brick walls managed to keep the unlit house of God bearable. One ceiling globe light was on, but another two just next to it were out, and plaster was starting to separate from the fresco angelic ceiling again after countless repairs. The aroma of burnt candles, incense, flowers, musty prayer books, and decades of wood polish combined to produce a heady but comforting scent.

The uneven wood floors snapped and squeaked with each footstep. Hidden in various corners and niches were saints to pray to for special favors. In the choir loft a woman was practicing on the ill-tuned organ, but she could never seem to get the notes to harmonize, much less the tempo. At different intervals in the music a female voice would begin to strain—a more accurate term than *sing*—which only further confirmed that the high pitch came from very aged vocal chords. Father Flariety was in the confessional box while six elderly ladies stood in line, some whispering and others pinching rosary beads. They turned in exact unison as the front door creaked open and shut with a bang.

A man stood there. He refused to look at the altar where the red glow of the sanctuary lamp flickered. His thick, dark and gray hair looked as though he had been in a windstorm and his beard had to be three days old. While his body was tawny and still somewhat solid despite lost weight, his appearance was dated by a half-open sport shirt and the T-shirt beneath. Even worse, he needed to tuck one side of his shirt back into his khaki pants. Street-worn tennis shoes finished his attire. For a moment the intruder seemed to be sizing up the situation as he checked out all the statues. He had prayed to every one of them, but they were deaf or didn't seem the least bit interested in his petition. He started toward the altar, hesitated, turned, and walked over to the confessional line.

The women knew what street people were like, and he was not that. But even more unnerving was the thought, *What if he is a mental case?* As the inky depth of his eyes began to look them over, one woman left the file and made for the door. Then he opened his mouth and smiled—and the atmosphere became ominous. Another woman left. Then all the ladies broke ranks and proceeded out the door. He swept back the faded velvet confessional curtain and a small boy on his knees let out a weak yelp. The man grabbed the boy by his collar and yanked him out of the box.

"I forgive you—get out."

As the man knelt, he heard the boy's running footsteps and the church door slam. He was alone with the priest.

"Bless me, Father, for I have sinned."

"Oh no! Not again, Bill!" A hint of Irish brogue was just caught within the words. "You can't keep doing this, my son. You simply must stop. Besides you're running my customers off. Get a hold of yourself, man!"

"Give it to me, Father. Give it to me, damn you! Do you want me to beg? Okay, I'm begging... Can't you see I have to have it for God's sake?"

"I can't do it. No one will, not even the bishop. He forbids it. All I can do is pray and bless you, Bill."

"It's not good enough! Nothing is working. It's my only

hope. I know it will—"

"My answer is final. I do not do exorcisms. I don't know how, and I don't know of any priest who does. That's the stuff of the Middle Ages and movies. Now is that clear, Bill? No, no, no!"

"You're as worthless as this church."

The priest heard the kneeler creak and the drape sweep open as the man left the box. He peeked through his curtain and he could see the man's shaking hand as he tried to light a votive candle underneath a faded plaster statue of Mary. Most of the votive glass containers were empty.

The clergyman looked up at the crucifix just above the sliding screen opening to the confessional box and spoke to it, "Please let him leave."

Then a loud snap and the smashing of glass were heard within the church.

"What the hell...?"

Father Flariety threw the half door back, at the same time thrusting the curtain aside, and emerged from the cubical. "How dare you? This is the Lord's house! Get out! Get out now, Bill Hughes!"

The man standing before the statue was covering his face with both hands as the smashed glass votive pieces sparkled on the marble floor.

The elderly priest was limping and the curvature of his spine made his back seem as if a hump was trying to protrude through his black robe. His cane thumped the floor toward the sacrilegious intruder.

"Oh Bill, what am I gonna do with you, my son? What am I gonna do?" His anger quickly turned to sympathy. "Here sit down."

The disturbed man collapsed onto the pew and Father Flariety eased his tortured body onto the wood next to him.

"My God, I'm lost. I'm in hell, Father."

"Bill, I can doctor your soul, but it's your mind that needs cleansing, my son. Surely you see that, my boy. This has nothing to do with exorcism or supernatural voodoo stuff."

"I'm so scared, Father."

"Put your hands down and look me in the face." When the troubled man complied, he continued, "You look worse than the last time you were here. You need help now, Bill. Surely you can see that? You're simply torturing yourself needlessly."

Once more he covered his eyes. "I've given up on help. Where is the God who made me? I need him so much, Father."

"I'm going to make a phone call. He's a friend of mine and comes here every so often to Mass. He has an office here in town. But come to think of it, he told me he was retiring from his practice. But it's worth a call."

"You mean a shrink?"

"Yes. This doctor helped me through a very difficult period. I knew when I was ordained that I was not headed to the top of the list. This spine and short leg made me look like Quasimodo the bell ringer. They knew I couldn't be presented as a gleaming messenger of God, so they assigned me here over forty years ago. I watched my fellow seminarians move on to better and better parishes, then be promoted to monsignors. Still others went to Rome for studies. One even became a bishop. I watched this year after year. Then came Vatican Two and so many priests left, I thought for sure they would close this church and I would be given a somewhat better parish. But nothing came and a deep resentment and depression began to fester inside me. The bottle almost became my phantom of escape. I had lost all hope, you see, and hope is all a priest really has in the end. Dr. Hansom took control of me and straightened me up so to speak. With his care and Christ's grace, I became restored. I think I'm more at ease now than I ever could hope for—that is until you started coming around."

The agonized man brought his hands down from his face,

gave a smirk, and attempted to smile.

"Now I'm just a crumpled old friar with one ancient assistant, Sister Lilly, and she's losing her hearing, God bless her. She's driving me crazy too…she lost her teeth somewhere and she has me sniffing all over the place for the things. As far as my church, I imagine they'll close the place when they demand my retirement, but I think they are hoping the heavenly Father will sound the trumpets for me. Retirement is expensive you see, in the church account books. But I got off the point. Dr. Hansom helped me find a peace, Bill."

"Peace—it's a word, Father, not a reality."

"Just you wait here." The old friar patted Bill Hughes' leg and limped through the sacristy door. Muffled voices could be heard. A black-draped nun emerged with a broom and dust pan, did her glass sweeping duty without even looking his way, and disappeared back into the side door of the altar. Again he caught site of the burning crimson from the altar lamp and quickly turned away. It frightened him. After twenty minutes Father Flariety shuffled back into the pew.

"Now take this address and phone number I've written down. And for Christ's sake, please be there on time and in a suit or at least some nice clean clothes. You look like a disaster. I've seen you spruced up when you used to come here long ago. Sister Lilly and I will storm heaven for you, my son. Remember, have hope and faith. And I may regret saying this, but I'll be here for you."

# Chapter 2

And so, three days later, Bill Hughes swallowed his tough-guy pride, snuffed out his cigarette in the hall canister, and entered the office door. The reception room was empty except for a couple of chairs. Open cardboard boxes with files were unevenly stacked about the wall.

"Hello, anyone here? Is this Dr. Hansom's office?"

"Is that you, Mr. Hughes? Do come back. I'm just clearing out the file drawers and desk. Father Flariety called and said you would help me out by carrying some of my boxes."

"He did?"

The office was all but empty too. Two overstuffed, but deep-cushioned leather armchairs and a desk were the only furnishings. The file drawers were opened but mostly empty. One picture hung on the wall.

"Just kidding—sit down here, Mr. Hughes, and make yourself comfortable. We're all alone. I guess he told you I was hanging it up."

"Yes."

"Decade upon decade of trying to be of help, and now it seems like it has only been perhaps a few years. Good God, time indeed does take wing. Now I'm ready for some serious traveling about the world."

As Bill sat down, the well-used seat was comfortable and enveloped his body. His mental image of the often-joked-about psychiatrist's couch was notably absent from this room. The doctor was also old and worn, just like Father Flariety. He looked more Jewish than Catholic.

"Is that the Ten Commandments on the wall?"

"Yes, Mr. Hughes."

"Are you Jewish?"

"All the way! Look at this magnificent nose!"

"Funny, I thought Father Flariety said you attended services at his church."

"Oh, I do."

"Oh, he's converting you, huh?"

"Good heavens, no. But the old priest keeps right on trying. That drawer over there is stuffed with holy cards, rosary beads, medals, and pamphlets. He never lets up. We calm each other's souls from time to time, you see. Father Flariety is a very holy person you know. I often go see him when I need to unwind—and yes, we brain crackers also need comfort from time to time. Come to think about it, we probably need more help than our patients! But you see I take in all the religions, from Shinto to black magic, from Catholic to Pentecostal. One must make sure all the bases are covered when checkout time comes, don't you think?"

"Well, I..."

"Oh, just pulling your string, Mr. Hughes! Religions are a hobby of mine, plus it's been of great help on many of my past cases. Deity mindset and religious principles in a person's character are often the cause for inner struggles."

Bill could tell the doctor was trying to break the ice. He was easing his tensions, and he knew that Bill knew it. But it did calm some of his apprehension.

"But let's see if I can be of assistance to you in some way. Just relax for a moment and make yourself comfortable."

He opened a small wall cooler and handed his new patient a plastic bottle of lemon something.

"That's a nasty scar on the top of your hand, Mr. Hughes. Is it healing?"

"Yes. It's an old burn. I stupidly burned it on a truck's tailpipe awhile back."

"Try to drink this, Mr. Hughes. It's just a mild relaxer. It'll help ease any tension before we start. Take a deep breath, now exhale. Another, now exhale. Now start from the beginning—from where you feel was the origin of the problem. I need to know everything, and I mean everything. And don't stop till when you walked in my office. The day is yours. Now let's get started."

The troubled man sat there silently sizing up his adversary—or redeemer. He was ready for any mercy, any hope, and he knew his end was near if he did not at least give this complete stranger some chance of helping him. He was descending to the realm of total madness, just hanging on to the edge of the cliff.

"I'm retired, Doc. I'm just an old cop. A bullet put my leg out of commission a few years ago. It required a couple surgeries and several months of physical therapy, but at least I qualified for early retirement. I'm divorced, but my bachelor life has been good. We never had any kids. She worked and I worked. You know how it is, we just fell out of love."

"Let's not start that far back, Mr. Hughes, only how this particular situation came about. I mean, if you can possibly target what you feel initiated the problem. Is it okay if I call you Bill?"

"Oh sure. Let's see…well, after my retirement I joined the usual clubs. While I was rehabilitating, I had to back off on sports, but I discovered oil painting, of all things, which then somehow led me to become involved with classical music. Me, a flat-foot detective. But I loved it, Doc. Opera performances at the Met were too expensive, so I would go to smaller productions and the free chamber music concerts offered about town, which were paradise for me. I also became involved with Arthur Conan Doyle's Sherlock

Holmes stories. I'd loved them for years, and I guess an old policeman never wants to really let go of the hunt—it's too ingrained in us. So after I retired, Sherlock Holmes and Dr. Watson became my main interest—so much so, that I was invited to the Baker Street Irregulars meeting as a guest.

"You see the Irregulars were the first Sherlock Holmes fan club in the States. It began in 1934. Most of the members were kinda geeky, but I loved it. I became so enthralled that after a while I found I was becoming somewhat of a notoriety around the town because of my extensive knowledge of the famous detective. But my real focus was on one story, *The Hound of the Baskervilles*. I just couldn't get enough of that story. I studied it, read every book on the area, and began writing small articles for magazines. Suddenly I found I was being invited to give talks on the hound story. Even more surprisingly, I was making a little money by doing what I loved best. I started getting expense-paid trips to various Holmes organizations around the country. Some of my written studies even made their way to England. But I was disappointed—I never seemed to have the bucks to go to the city where the great detective lived, much less Dartmoor where the story had taken place."

"Go on, Bill...that's fine."

"I think it was last autumn, about November, when a foreign-stamped letter dropped out of my post office box. That elusive invitation had finally arrived. It was a request for me to give a series of lectures at Queens' College in Cambridge on the Baskerville story from an American point of view. I remember thinking, *At last! I've made it.* Oh, it was a small stipend for sure, but it included the travel costs, and I was ecstatic that I was going there. I suppose a policeman's pension wouldn't be so bad if this town wasn't so damn expensive. You see, I had my twenty-five years in, and I'd planned to retire at fifty-five anyway, if I hadn't been shot six years ahead of that. But as it is, I can barely vacation in the States, much less overseas. Some of my buddies have never even left New York."

"Let's stick to the point, Bill."

"Okay, okay. Let's see… Oh yeah, I realized Cambridge was pretty far north and east of the Devonshire district. That's where the Dartmoor wasteland is located and the Baskerville story took place. But what mattered was that I was going to England and somehow I would soak myself in everything Sherlockian. It was my great chance. I was going to Baker Street and certainly Dartmoor—come hell or high water—and nothing, short of being run over, could stand in my way.

"When I got to Queens' College, I met with the staff professor, plus his other junior teachers in the enrichment program. I was set up in a small room on the campus, escorted about the place, and then shown the town. I was given an introduction to the literary fiction class where I was to lecture. Basically it was how the Holmes stories were created and the history of the Baskerville chronicle. I loved it. The English countryside and the polite manners of the people seemed so civilized. And it was easy to see how the British landscape captured an artist; the range of colors just saturated one's eye. Hell, I never wanted to leave. But if you think New York is cold, try Cambridge in February."

"Yes, I know. I've been there in the winter."

"Then came one of those bank holidays that they have but we don't. So I took the train to London over the weekend and found all I wanted of the haunts and areas of Holmes. I even experienced a deep London fog. I was in heaven!

"When I went back to Queens' College they had some type of enormous power failure. Even the electrical wiring was ruined and there was no heat. I remember the staff was all upset—they were looking at possibly three weeks for the repairs. A few core classes were relocated, but all the rest were postponed, including mine. Well, since I wasn't needed, I decided to hop a train to Devon.

"It was a long trip. Then on top of that, I had to bus to the nearest town that was somewhere near the legendary Baskerville area. I just wanted to feel the atmosphere of the place. I knew Conan Doyle had gone there and stayed in Princetown, which sits right smack in the middle of the Dartmoor region. That's where he captured ideas for the *Hound of the Baskervilles* story. I wanted to get that charge that he may have found.

"Happily, I came across a small, family-style hotel called The Red Bull in a small community called Postbridge. Being off season, there was no problem getting accommodations. The hamlet the hotel sat in was but a few buildings and houses, but it also sat just about in the middle of Dartmoor. The village setting was right out of a movie script. The Red Bull even had a small pub attached to the dining room. I believe it only had maybe eight hotel rooms. I grabbed a bicycle from the inn and began to ride the lonely roads all over the moors.

"Doc, it was everything Doyle described. The vastness and feeling of empty loneliness was to the point of being overpowering. Of course I started writing about the experience—I saw some money coming my way when I returned to the States. As I peddled the bicycle along the empty roads, I would pull my tape player out of the backpack, stick in the ear phone, and become lost in Bizet's 'Intermezzo from Carmen.' See, Doc, I told you I knew my music."

"Yes, indeed you do."

"The composition only enhanced the measureless miles as I bumped along. Colors of raw umber, yellow oxides, and burnt reds mixed and swirled with vivid greens. There, as if guarding the whole moor, were huge stone boulders looking like carved watchtowers. There was also a line of winter trees that seemed friendly but then gave way as I crested a hill, and I found myself in a free glide down the road. I was cruelly ushered into a wasteland of wind-whipped gray and yellow grass. It was nothing short of an expanse of waving emptiness with protruding boulders and dotted, variegated flora sprinkled with some type of scrub vegetation that seemed more dead than alive. The ear concert tended to blend the whole vista into a mixture of checks and balances with the green of the living, the dried sticks of the past, and the cold stone of the dead.

"Old Mr. Saunders and his wife who owned the inn seemed like mother and father figures to me, and the small village was tidy and clean. Many of the pub regulars even called me 'Yank.' I took it as kind of a compliment. The guests in the room next door to mine were the Cartwrights: Peter, his wife Mary, and their son Roddy. The kid was sort of an up-and-coming rock star, and they were there to set up some type of music video like you see on television. Something like the rock star promotions that are becoming the rage, only it was a British version. At that point they were just biding their time as the video crew had not arrived yet. They told me over breakfast one morning how the film director was going to have their 'talented' son do a movie shoot over the moors with him jumping around off crag rocks or something like that. Hell, he looked like a freak to me, all that green hair junk and pins sticking out of his lips and nose. I can honestly say I never took up with them too much. But they were likable enough. They said for me to remember them if I came to London—they liked the American cop adventures. God forbid, telling cop stories, that's all I needed.

"A reverend and his wife had the other room down the hall. They seemed a bit younger than me and she seemed like the quiet type. His name was Carl and his wife was Jennifer, but he called her Jenny. Their last name was Williamson. There was another man down the hall, but I didn't see him while I was settling in.

"I think it was about the second day I met the local constable, John Clayton. Clayton was sort of a simple guy—he was better suited for the country. Heck, even I could tell he would have never made it in the city. Clayton was more like a British version of our backwoods, country boy type of deputy. He and I got on because of our law enforcement kinship, and he always wanted to know about the gangsters in New York. I lied a lot because I was mostly assigned to the normal homicide cases in a precinct, but I acted like I was somehow connected to the organized crime bureau. He would always jump away from any discussion of Doyle's Sherlock Holmes Baskerville story. He laughed it off, as did the innkeeper couple. As I think back on it, the regular patrons never seemed responsive to any of my questions about the story. I guess they had been saturated with it all their lives.

"But then they did get serious when someone mentioned that some sheep plus a few wild moor ponies had been attacked and killed not three months before I arrived. Officer Clayton said he had shot two wild dogs and thought that would have put a stop to the marauding. But only a few days before I arrived, another two sheep were found with their throats torn out and mauled. Clayton was going to try to set up some meat traps to get the rest of the dog pack.

"Mr. Saunders, the owner, said that every few years the wild dogs about the moors would seem to pack up and would have to be eliminated. Of course I brought up the Baskerville hound scenario—but he laughed it off. He had heard it over and over during his years in the village and from other Sherlock Holmes fan club members. He said that the Sherlock Holmes stuff would, at times, really help business in the small hamlet, but sheep killing was serious business to the local farmers. They were not to be trifled with if livestock carnage or stealing was involved.

"Those first nights in Dartmoor were everything a novel cried for, Doc: the deep mists, then the wind-driven rains, nights so dark that the outdoor lights outside the inn couldn't penetrate the gloom. I walked out along the paths, but I always felt a little uncomfortable. Besides, they warned me about certain areas that were mushy, like our quicksand, and—just as Doyle wrote—could swallow a person up if one wasn't careful. The moor also had spectacular parts with easy rolling hills, but as I said, other areas were bleak and haunting, exactly as Dr. Watson described in his letters to Holmes during his stay at Baskerville Hall.

"During the first days, besides bicycling I would take lunch in a small pack, strap on my walking boots, and roam around. Most of the paths were easy to walk as they were old and well worn. During the long walks I could see a few farm houses in the distance, and one day I came across a small travel trailer and a couple of Range Rovers parked near a large tent. Three men seemed to be digging.

"*God*, I thought, *this is just like the real Baskerville story*, when Dr. Watson met the novel's villain, Stapleton, out on the moor. I introduced myself, and in turn the man in charge offered his hand in friendship, as did the others. The leader of the group was an archeologist, Professor Harold Latimer, and the other two were his associates, John Spensor and Barney Stockdale. I recall noticing at the time that Stockdale was extremely small, almost like a horse jockey. He was busy scraping around a rock that lay in a small ditch. Stakes and strings marked the work zone. Spensor was the opposite of Stockdale. He was muscular and appeared to keep to himself as he pushed a wheelbarrow of dirt to the screen box used for sifting. They were trying to uncover what they felt was perhaps a large gathering hall of the early Bronze Age period. Like in the Doyle story of the hound, there were sites of early human stone settlements about the whole rolling landscape.

"Professor Latimer had a thick set of almost pure white hair. I particularly remember, Doc, that he seemed to be in his mid-fifties and was lean from what must have been years of digging. He was kind enough to show me what they had uncovered: bone fragments, what he said were stone working implements, plus stained earth where charcoal indicated a cooking area. He said the site was going to be important and he and the others were excited about the discovery. I asked if he had any students to help, and he said that he expected some during the summer but was now having to get along with his small work party. Around the camp were various digging apparatus, plus a small tool shed that held welding implements. A curly haired, mongrel dog lounged under the open air shed uncaring about the whole operation. I stayed there about an hour, as well as I can remember. Latimer offered me a ride back to the village as he was going into Princetown to pick up some groceries.

*"Not too safe out here at night, Mr. Hughes. There have been some wild dogs about lately. Besides, the bog areas are extremely dangerous, you know."*

"I told Latimer I certainly understood, as those words were already ingrained by the warning pamphlet the innkeeper gave me and by Clayton the constable—and of course I couldn't pass up the comment, *'And the big bad wolf, too!'* It brought on a nice bit of laughter during our road trip back to the hotel, and I explained my objective of being on the moors. He rambled on about how the funding was much more generous for archeological hunting here than in other sites about England.

"It was so cold when the professor dropped me off, and I recall plunging into a hot beef pie at the pub. After a brandy I brought my notebook down from the room to my small dining booth and began writing an account of the day for future reference. The reverend and his wife, the only ones in the eating area, were having tea and conversing with Mrs. Saunders. Eventually the clergyman retired upstairs and his wife was left alone with her thoughts in front of the snapping and popping hearth. Old man Saunders kept serving the stout to some farmers in the adjoining pub, and the cracking fire with the few mumbling customers made for what I saw as the perfect British night.

"After a while I watched the reverend's wife meander over to the old upright piano, which sat just inside the restaurant part of the hotel. Doc, it was as if magic happened. She casually went into the first movement of Beethoven's well-known 'Moonlight Sonata,' and the old ivory keys—with some terribly out of pitch—sounded like a concert grand at Carnegie Hall. She looked as if she'd left us all and entered into her own world. Everyone came to the doorway and stood there in awe and respectful silence. The soft spell of the music seemed just right for the solemn moor night. She was a vision, Doc. Her loveliness meshed in the classic arrangement was making me want her, if you know what I mean. The moors, the small hotel, her beauty, and the music—this place was the Land of Oz as far as I was concerned. I never wanted the day to end.

"Then she just stopped. Everyone clapped, causing her to be startled as she had evidently lost herself in the composition. She twisted around on the stool and thanked the small audience.

*"Please go on, ma'am,"* Mrs. Saunders pleaded as she wiped her hands on her apron.

*"I've forgotten how the rest of it goes."*

*"Maybe I can find some music later in the closet and you can play for us after dinner?"*

*"I'll try, Mrs. Saunders."*

*"Oh marvelous! I haven't heard that old piano play in years."*

"Slowly the small audience retreated back into the pub, Doc, and she began to perform another selection. I recognized it as a Mozart piece, but this time she was in a sweet and intimate state—the keys were barely audible. Again she was unable to complete the composition. Next came Rodgers and Hammerstein's "You'll Never Walk Alone," which was played almost like a waltz, bringing back some of the tavern fellows. Then, after having to stop because of forgotten notes, she began once more. Mr. Saunders, wiping a glass with a bar towel, stood behind her and began to sing the words. Then some of the other patrons joined in. After the selection finished they all clapped, thanked her again, and a glass of wine was brought to her from the bar in appreciation. The patrons once more retreated back into the pub section.

"Mrs. Williamson started to sweep the keys with something soothing again that I couldn't recognize. I was mesmerized and just let both her stunning beauty and music absorb into me. I had visions of grabbing her right off the piano seat and making love to her. I was also trying to figure out just how to meet her, but she seemed such a private person. I did notice that she would quit for a moment, look over toward my table, give a small smile, then go back to where she was trying to remember the rest of the sonata.

"Finally she stopped all together, stood up, and looked out the window. She couldn't see anything, just her reflection in the onyx black glass. Only a dim solitary street light managed to twinkle in the distance. It was like a lonely star. She seemed to be so absorbed in her thoughts, and I wanted to know those thoughts, Doc. What could she possibly be thinking? I wanted to know not only her body but her mind. That damn red, glowing hair was so long, and it made me want even more to know if her female hair down in her thighs was as flaming hot. Hell, Doc, I was becoming so wrapped up in her—she was like a lightning bolt that struck into my whole being. Then when I looked down at my notes and again glanced to where she stood, she was gone.

"Damn, Doc, I wondered at the time, *Why didn't I say even a word to her?* Or even a more vain thought, *Why didn't she come over to my booth?* I had lost the moment."

# Chapter 3

"The next night I was writing my notes at my regular table, just sort of scribbling some ideas for a magazine article, when I noticed the reverend and his wife in a deep conversation by the fire. They seem to be quietly arguing, Doc, if you know what I mean, and I heard him call her Jenny. Good God, she was one good-looking woman. How he ever got her beats me."

"Let's keep to the subject, Bill." Dr. Hansom shifted his position in his chair.

"Okay. Well, she got up abruptly and went upstairs, and I just went back to putting some ideas together. Then the light was blocked from my paper and when I looked up the good reverend was standing over me with his cup of tea. It was a wild evening and the wind gusts beat at the window panes to be let inside.

*"I hope I'm not bothering you, Mr. Hughes?"*

*"Oh no, just jotting down some thoughts. And call me Bill, Reverend."*

*"And mine is Carl, Bill."* He held out his hand and we clasped.

*"My wife was a little tired this evening so she is off to bed. You see, I thought it would be nice for her to hide away here for a small vacation while I went to boring church meetings in Exeter. She needs the rest, poor darling. But the reason why I came over to bother you was that Mr. Saunders told me you're here on a lecture tour about Sherlock Holmes and Sir Conan Doyle?"*

*"Well, I'm really supposed to be at Cambridge, but the school's power failed and it's given me the opportunity to make a visit here to Dartmoor."*

*"Been here before, Bill?"*

*"No."*

*"It's everything Doyle wrote about and more if you ask me—my wife loves it, but the place depresses me for sure. But you know, as I was driving back today, I was wondering about the old legend of the Baskerville dog."*

*"You mean the hound, Carl?"*

*"Oh yes, the hound. Funny how an American—not to be presumptuous—would be a Holmes expert."*

*"Oh, I don't know. Did you know that the American Civil War has more of an interest here than back in the States? Many, many learned men abound here who can put American historians to shame. It just all depends upon one's interests."*

*"Rightly so, Mr. Hughes—I mean Bill."* He paused. *"Could you by chance, I mean if it's not too much of a bother, enlighten me on the Baskerville history aspect? Would be nice to relate it to Jenny, and I am curious myself."*

*"Please sit down."*

"He nestled into the booth opposite me and began stirring his tea.

*"Actually it goes back to around the 1600's and even a bit earlier as well, as I recollect. It seems there was a mythical hunter called the Dewier. This Dewier was a terrible fellow. He killed at random, whether it be beast or man, and he had a pack of dogs called Whist hounds that were as mean as himself. They were said to have bright red eyes. Also, it was a mistake to follow the dogs because they*

would lead one over a cliff on the moor, or even worse, plunge one into a bottomless bog or pool."

"That's interesting."

"Back then the clergymen used the Dewier myth to encourage the locals to head to church and have their babies baptized."

"What does baptism have to do with the dogs—I mean the hounds?"

"Well, the mean old Dewier and the dogs' favorite food was un-baptized babies."

"My word!"

"I think it was just another way to get the tithes myself."

"Capital! I might try it!"

"Ah, but there's more, Reverend. It seems there was a 'Black Dog' myth too. While the Whist canines would patrol the roads and attack evening strollers about the moor, even worse was one hound that was called the 'Black Dog of Dartmoor.' This mastiff would go so far as to chase carriages and horsemen and was known to snatch a rider off his horse for a snack."

"That's absolutely marvelous, Bill, I so love the folk legend side of it. But where does the Baskerville curse come in? I mean everybody knows Doyle's story, but is there any connection to a real family?"

"Well, it's a known fact by Holmes enthusiasts that there was a man named Bertram Fletcher Robinson. He was a journalist whom Doyle played golf with. During a game a heavy rain drove them inside the Royal Links Hotel, and after a few cocktails Robinson began to relate the stories of a legendary 'Black Shuck.' Basically it was a hound that roamed the Norfolk region. Robinson then went on to the tales of Dartmoor's hounds. I can imagine after a few more scotch cocktails the tales got even more interesting."

"I would bet so...but was there an actual family thing?"

"Well, the biographers of Doyle claim that finally Robinson related the basic story that gave Doyle the punch to get on with the famous mystery. Robinson mentioned a man by the name of Squire Richard Cabell, who had lived in the area around the 1600's or 1700's. One expert dated it concisely as 1677. Well, the old squire suspected that his wife was stepping out on him. He finally had it out with her and she fled from the house. There she was hell bent for leather—oops! That's an old cowboy term for really moving out."

"Oh, I see."

"As I said, she ran out and fled across the moors and alongside of her was her faithful dog. Cabell went after her and caught up with the unfaithful girl and gave her such a beating that she collapsed dead near one of those granite boulders. The pet hound was wild with anger and then assaulted the squire by ripping out his throat. But the squire got in a few licks too, and the hound finally expired from stab wounds. Henceforth the woman's pet stalked the Cabell family line."

"Fantastic, Bill, really first rate. Anything else?"

"I guess there is this. Conan Doyle and Robinson became even better friends, and some Holmes people say that they began to collaborate on the story with both men roaming the moors together. Robinson would point out features that were unique, while Doyle figured how to place them in the story. Their car driver was named Harry Baskerville, so it doesn't take a rocket scientist to see where

41

that ended up in the story. Robinson bowed out in some way and Doyle continued on. When first writing it, Sherlock Holmes was not involved, but Doyle woke up and found it would be a perfect fit to the legend. Doyle even had a map in the story that showed the location of Baskerville Hall, you know."

"Really? I of course read the thing, but I guess I must not have had a copy showing the map."

"If you get Doyle's map of the moor, Baskerville Hall was located just southeast of Princetown, between here and Whiteworks, which is south of us. But really it was closer to Princetown. The fictitious town of Grimpen in the Baskerville story, according to The Annotated Sherlock Holmes book, might have been Widecombe, which is close to us. Doyle jumbled all the locations together to fit the story. But it's so interesting to see the places that he might have visited for the novel. At least it is for me."

"Unbelievable. I never would have guessed. Any other juicy stuff?"

"There is a bit more trivia. Seems that Fletcher Robinson later on went delving into the famous legend of a certain 'mummy's curse.'"

"You've got to be kidding?"

"No, no, he started to investigate various stories about mysterious events that would happen to archeologists who dug and studied the Egyptian sites. Lo and behold if Robinson didn't become sick. And before he completed his research he caught typhoid fever and died."

"Oh, come on. You're pulling my leg now, old fellow."

"Check it out yourself. As a matter of fact, even Conan Doyle said upon Robinson's death that he had *warned him about prying into unknown things and that he was tempting fate. But Robinson didn't pay attention and he was only thirty-five when he was struck down."*

*"Good Lord!"*

"I recall there was momentary break, Doc, as the pastor tried to soak in the legendary events versus the actual facts. He never sipped his tea but just kept stirring the beige liquid. He never let loose from his air of superfluous sophistication. He sat straight up like a store mannequin the entire time.

*"Anything going on nowadays, Bill?"*

*"No...but old man Saunders told me just in the last few months a larger than normal amount of sheep and ponies that roam wild about the moor have been found dead and—"*

*"Don't tell me. They had their throats torn out like the legends."*

*"You guessed it. But he says every so often some wild dogs will pack up and cause the ruckus. They hunt them down and then all things settle back to normalcy. Only this time they can't seem to catch the rascals. Even worse, a local lawman said some of the domestic stock have been attacked, and not just out on the moor, but inside the sheep and cattle pens, too."*

*"Good God, that sounds scary—better tell Jenny to be careful on her solitary jaunts."*

*"Might be a good idea for her to not travel too far down the paths."*

*"Well, I'm all out of it. Please excuse me for the stretch, but my constitution, as they say, has announced it's time for my retirement. But I can't thank you enough for taking time to give me a part of the local fables. I'm afraid my lecture would not be quite as daring for sure. Do*

*American policeman practice the faith on a regular basis?"*

*"Oh yes, more than you think, or are led to think on the television and movies. The movies always tend to show a tough-guy approach, but every time one has to enter an unknown building the prayers are faithfully on the lips."*

*"That's comforting to know. Well, many thanks again and sleep well, Bill. See you at breakfast."*

*"Good night, Carl, until the morning."*

"I couldn't figure him out, Doc. I knew he must be younger than me, but somehow I felt like he spoke to me as a parent or teacher might humor a child. He was very proper and polite, but it was more than just the usual British way. He seemed stuffy to me. As I watched him disappear up the steps, I wondered how she slept with him, and what kind of raw love he could give to such a stunning woman. He just didn't look as if he was worthy of her, Doc. In my mind I was the one who could make her groan with more lust than she could stand, not him. Then all was quiet and I found myself suddenly all alone in the dining room. The log fire had all but exhausted itself. The pub was also silent.

"Doc, I can still see the last of those hearth embers die away. I can remember it because of one reason."

"What reason was that, Bill?"

"Because when I turned to look out the window into the windstorm, I almost had a heart attack. The fire coals perfectly reflected onto a glass pane, and two red-hot eyes looked straight into mine. I can tell you everything skipped a beat."

# Chapter 4

"The next morning I bicycled to a place called Grimspound. There were early ruins at the site and it was a locale Conan Doyle had visited for the story. It's more of a Neolithic settlement with a clump of boulders, which Dr. Watson mentions in the Baskerville story. It was about a three mile ride and the morning was crisp and cold. I remember I really couldn't stay long as the bitter wind was going right through me, so I rode back.

"I arrived just in time to see Jenny heading north across the road and along a path that headed to the Fox Tor Mire area. That moor was really not a safe place. At the same time, her husband honked the horn of his car for a friendly wave as he pulled out of the hotel drive. He was no doubt going to Exeter for more church meetings. I don't know why, Doc, but I didn't like the scenario—it was a cop instinct or something, so I followed the woman. She went deeper and deeper into the moor, never even looking back.

"Finally, after a good hour, she came to the bog part of the moor. I recall she stood there for what seemed like fifteen minutes then went back up to a small outcrop of rocks and sat down. It was freezing, I can tell you that for sure. I pretended I was taking the path also and waved at her as I rounded a granite boulder and made my way to her perch.

*"Are you all right? I mean you seem to be really farther out than most of the folks I've seen in the last few days."*

*"Oh yes, I'm fine. Here sit down. It's nice and dry*

*here on the stone. You're Mr. Hughes, aren't you? Carl was telling me about how you educated him on the Baskerville story."*

*"Oh, it's really the same old fictitious story wrapped around the legend of a lonely dog. But please, call me Bill."*

*"Of course, and mine is Jenny."* She paused. *"Bill— my father's name was Bill. It's such a warm name."*

*"Well, I'm just plain old Bill."*

"I made her chuckle a little and it warmed the mood.

*"Can I tell you how much I loved your playing Beethoven and the other songs? I was so enraptured with you doing that by memory."*

*"Oh, for Lord's sake, I was stumbling awkwardly. It's been awhile since I've sat down and played."*

*"I loved it."*

"I tried to say it intensely and in a soft meaningful way. I knew she caught my sincerity. The woman then seemed to let go of a smile and gave me such a sweet look into my eyes, Doc, I could have stood there stark naked and never felt the cold.

*"My goal as a young girl was to storm the classical stage and hopefully become a concert pianist. Dad even hired me a teacher well into college, but then I met Carl while he was studying music for his ministry. And so I gave it up and became a minister's wife. How did you become so acquainted that you knew what I was playing—or should I say attempting to play?"*

*"Get ready for this. I played the tapes in the squad car when I was in New York. Pretty well drove my partners crazy."*

*"You're a policeman?"*

*"I was. Now I'm thankfully retired and write on subjects related to the Conan Doyle stories. I'm doing a*

*small lecture series at Cambridge at this time, but a temporary malfunction of the school's power station has given me a few weeks of freedom. So here I am and in your company."*

*"Yes, I have my freedom here too. Sounds horrible, but Carl's once-a-year meetings give me a chance to be alone with myself. A reverend's wife is as public as a grocery store. How I love this place—even the cold is friendly."*

*"Yes. I understand. Yet it's also ominous in a way. I hear a lot of animals on the moor often get stuck in the mud pools and drown. But perhaps I should leave you alone and get on..."*

*"Oh no, please don't go. It's wonderful to talk to someone who is a stranger and loves the classics. Our congregation isn't of that vein. They're more into just hymnals. I feel that sometimes my husband's church is in a desert and the masterpieces are an oasis for me. Oh, I shouldn't be speaking like that... Forgive me."*

*"I can understand."*

"She quickly broke off the subject. She pointed her finger toward a hazy blue, distant hillside.

*"What's that, Bill? Look out there, just beyond that rock cluster. I can barely make out an individual walking; looks like a pony or sheep is following some ways back. Can you see? It's there, you can just make it out. Now it's only the person."*

*"Yes, I can see—now he's gone. He is way out there isn't he? Brave hiker in that mushy area."*

"We didn't say anything for a while. Then she came out with her thoughts.

*"Do you ever wonder how it was when people lived*

47

*here so many centuries ago? I mean they could go and come as they pleased. I'd like to think they never had any concern about social standings or had to live up to pretentious standards. I hope they were wild and free as the wild moor ponies. At least that's how I want to envision them."*

*"Yes, they were indeed free to roam, but I'm sure their existence was not very cozy, and short lived at that."*

"She said nothing Doc, but I could see her eyes just begin to glaze.

*"What makes you think our existence is any better? They were free and we live in a civilized zoo. We look at one another from our own cages."*

*"True, Jenny, but we are comfortable in those cages. They were just surviving and living on the edge so to speak."*

"She looked away from me and back toward the distant hill that was capped with umber gray boulders. The rocks lay jumbled as if thrown haphazardly there by a giant's hand.

*"I live there, you know. I mean in a cage."*

"A cold wind then whipped us both and her hair swirled wildly as she tried to keep it from her eyes.

*"I felt that was the case Jenny—I can tell it a bit."*

*"I know you can. People who possess a music or art instinct have a better understanding of feelings and the passion of life. I really believe that. When I saw you look over at me after playing the piano I could tell you were in that delicate group. Carl and I don't get along very well, and it's showing more every day. Even his parishioners are now tuned in. Oh, it's not his fault. He warned me twenty years ago, before we married, that the life of a reverend's wife was a sacrifice. Clergy wives were always to be in the social thick of it, he said. It turned out to be so true. I never was the type to come out—we've been to three different churches and*

*I never seem to fit in. How I could have ever had visions of being a stage pianist beats me—I don't seem to like crowds even in church. God knows I've tried—I even prayed for an escape. I know Carl needs me, but I just don't have the social skills that his ministry requires. I'm always on the outside."*

*"Yeah, when I got my divorce I fell right in that mode. I was miserable. But you'll find the answer, Jenny. I promise that it comes in time."*

*"But you see, I don't have much time."*

*"What do you mean? Are you ill?"*

*"No, not physically. Maybe mentally."*

"She tried to laugh it off, but she gulped a bit to try and control her emotions. I really think she wanted to cry so badly, but she held herself together.

*"I've all but ruined my husband's career. You see, I was so out of touch that I fell in love with another man. We did the unspeakable for a reverend's wife. Those things never can hide themselves and eventually Carl found out, but he's been so stoic about it all. God, it is so awful. The whole thing is awful."*

"She turned her face away from me and again composed herself.

*"I don't know why I'm making you hear this sob story, Mr. Hughes."*

*"Bill, Jenny."*

*"I mean Bill. Let's talk about something else."*

*"Let's not, Jenny. We all need to let things flow at times. Remember I'm that stranger that you could talk to. What better could you ask for? I used to do it all the time when I was a city cop. Didn't even know a guy—maybe he was just a streetwise thug, but it felt good after I had vented.*

That's what the psychiatrists call letting it all out—venting."

"I see."

"Her voice was so gentle, Doc. Hell, I was falling in love with her. That blazing red hair seemed to brighten and was blowing around her face and shoulders then accenting itself against the colors of the brown moor. I can see her now, that skin color was even more heightened by the wind. Damn, she was so ripe, I really loved her."

"Get on with it, Bill," the doctor shifted his position.

"I said to her:

*"Jenny, you need to maybe see someone who can really help you."*

*"Oh, Carl has said that too, but I can't now—it's deeper than you think."*

*"Why so deep, Jenny? Hell, we all need changes. Maybe you need to get away from Carl and the congregation for a while. Go be with the guy you fell in love with, or back with your family, but don't go into depression for God's sake. It's not worth it."*

*"I can't do what you say, I mean leave Carl for the other man."*

*"Why not?"*

*"Because the man I loved was killed in an auto accident. It happened well over a year ago, but it wasn't until recently when his wife was sorting through his private papers that she learned about us. She talked to Carl, and somehow the whole congregation found out, and it became an awful scandal. That's why I came here. I knew Carl would be away during the day and I could try and grab hold. You see, I have recently been in a facility...you see...in other words, a mental house...and Carl is desperately trying to understand the whole mess."*

*"Jesus, Jenny, I'm so very sorry."*

*"I'm now alone even more. Jim is gone. I've ruined Carl's ambitions. I have nothing to go to, nowhere to start over."*

*"Your parents or children could perhaps help."*

*"We have no children, and why should I ruin my parents' lives? Besides, they had aspirations of me becoming a concert pianist in the first place and weren't too fond of Carl. But love conquers, and so we married."*

"She was becoming colder in the face. Not the body cold, Doc, but the lack of emotion coldness one sees. I mean she steeled herself and the wanting to cry just suddenly went away.

*"Can we go back now, Bill? I'm getting rather frigid."*

*"Of course, Jenny."*

*"Please don't talk to Carl, will you?"*

*"Of course not."*

"Doc, we walked back to the inn and just made small talk, so to speak. It was so wonderful for me, but for her it was as if she was in complete despair. I loved her so much at that time that it hurt. I guess it was her face, the place, her music, the moment, her revealed feelings, and her hopelessness. I envisioned myself trying to help her, even taking her away with me. It all came together and just boiled inside me. Damn, I wanted her. I wanted to save her, Doc. I really wanted her to be happy with me and no one else."

# Chapter 5

"That's quite understandable, Bill. We want to help beautiful things, it's in our nature. But do go on."

"It was the next day, a Tuesday I think. No, it was a Wednesday—hell, I don't remember."

"It's not necessary, just relax and tell the story on any time level."

"The following day was so warm, it seemed almost like a spring morning compared to the chill of the previous day. Of course I looked for Jenny at breakfast as Mrs. Saunders came in the small dining area with coffee.

*"Seen Mrs. Williamson this morning, Mrs. Saunders?*

*"No, I haven't. Maybe she went into town with the reverend?"*

*"Yes. I was hoping for more music."*

"Of course I was lying through my teeth, but it sounded good enough.

*"Yes, she is a talented girl. Now what can I fix you for breakfast, Mr. Hughes?"*

"Again I planned a trek on the moor, but because it wasn't very cold I wanted to go deeper in the forbidden garden. Doyle called this location a 'melancholy moor.' Actually it was south of the inn toward a vast and windy plain of few trees and colorless grasses spotted with patches of green and an outcropping of boulders. On the map it read 'Abbot's Way.'

"Mrs. Saunders packed me a small lunch and I was off. God, Doc, I can still see the countryside. So magnificent in the late morning light, but I could see where Conan Doyle could interpret the place as sinister by night. The silence and wind were my only companions and again a few unknown birds squeaked and fluttered from the turf. The always vigilant crows or ravens patrolled the sky making sure I was not their enemy. Their warning calls punctuated the moor wind gusts. The path was dry so I was able to move along at a good clip. Eventually I lost sight of the inn; then the country roadway vanished. I knew that just off the trail might be one of those mires that the innkeeper warned me about as I hiked on. Just farther ahead lay a rather large hill, and I finally topped it after almost a half hour walk.

"As I sat on a perfectly flat rock that seemed to be almost manmade, I began to wonder if I had lost the very reason why I came to Dartmoor—I was finding myself more affected by Jenny than by any Sherlock Holmes fantasy. I was wrapped up in a married woman, but one who hardly even noticed me because of her pain. More thoughts and absurd reasoning about her mixed and churned in my brain.

"Suddenly I heard a yell from behind me and quickly turned in that direction. Doc, I was blessed. Hell, it was Jenny actually running up the hill path toward me! God, I was so unbelievably happy. But then as she came closer, her voice and waving arms seemed more of a panic exertion than any imaginary attraction toward me.

*"Bill! Thank God it's you! Please hurry, it's a matter of life and death. Oh please..."*

*"Of course. What's the matter?"*

*"Come on please. I'll explain as we run."*

*"For God's sake Jenny, is someone dying?"*

*"Yes!"*

"Doc, running in heavy walking shoes was like jogging in the army again. I'd worked hard to get back in shape after the surgeries, but my leg just doesn't work as well as it used to. She was easily ahead of me. Hell, I had to stop a few times, but her constant prompting made me feel ashamed that I wasn't the man she needed.

*"Come on Bill, hurry! Oh please...you've got to save them!"*

*"Save who? Who's in trouble?"*

"Once again she was far ahead and a rush of wind disguised her voice as she turned and answered my question. Then she went quickly up a small rise and disappeared at the top. As I peaked the hill, I saw her kneeling at a small greenish circle. She was screaming like a wild woman. There were two dirty figures just in front of her.

*"For Christ's sake, Bill, hurry! Damn it, hurry!"*

"As I came down the path I stumbled once and again charged toward her. Something gray and muddy brown was moving back and forth. Precariously she was trying to lunge at it. When I finally came to her, I was breathing so hard I thought my heart and lungs were coming through my chest. Just out of the reach of her arms were the churning bodies of two sheep stuck in the deadly muck, and with each twist the two went further down. For some reason I noticed extremely large marks—what seemed to be some kind of animal prints—all around the edge of the mushy pool. *Had something chased the sheep into the watery death trap?* But Jenny's shriek awoke me from the observation.

*"Oh, for God's sake, do something!"*

"I then noticed that one was larger and the other just a mere lamb. But both were almost black with the miry goo.

*"What the hell?"*

*"Help them, Bill....do something, damn it! It's a mother and her lamb."*

*"How the hell did—?"*

54

*"Oh, I don't know. Either the baby got stuck and the mother went to it or vice versa... Can't you do something, Bill? You must!"*

"I looked around for any type of log that I could use to throw into the grimy pool, but the ground was only covered in some kind of marshy looking grass. Nothing was there. Then the whine of the bigger sheep was answered by the baby. The grip was tightening and pulling them. Steam was frothing from their mouths and even coming off the animals. The exhaustive struggle and dire situation pointed at an inevitable end.

"Jenny suddenly lay down and began to crawl over the mush but sank as she again desperately reached for the young lamb.

*"No, Jenny....no! Damn it, you'll go too!"*

*"I've got to try. I have too!"*

"Her heavy coat was drenched in mud and her arms slid all the way into the sludge.

*"Damn it, get back Jenny!"*

"I pulled her feet and accidently slipped down as she was released from the deadly pond.

*"Bill, please....oh please!"*

"She was crying and her words became nothing but heaves of sobs, her muddy mittens covered her face. She was on her knees now and didn't want to look at the agony just feet away. The mud transferred from her gloves to her face.

"Then the mother sheep began to bawl, and you know, Doc, it was almost like a human crying. The baby was also answering its mother, and Jenny's uncontrollable yelling only intensified the helplessness of the freakish moment.

*"Do something, Bill...do something!"*

"I instinctively took off my coat and decided to make it a cushion on the slime. Maybe, just maybe, it would make a temporary buoyant platform. Then Jenny stood up, uncovered, and threw her coat on top of mine.

*"Jenny, grab hold of my ankles when I lie down and hold on as tight as possible."*

*"Yes Bill, yes."*

"Doc, I slid out onto the coats about as far as my waist, and I was going down. The cold water slid over the coat, then seeped through my sweater and finally into my shirt. Then the T-shirt soaked up the cold mush and engulfed the warmth of my skin. God, the warmish day was suddenly frigid. The young puffing lamb was closest to me and I lunged as hard as I could but missed. This effort only made the two sheep more desperate and they again tried to free themselves, but they only went deeper. The mother was now up to the top of her legs and the poor lamb was already starting to be covered over.

*"Get the baby, Bill! For God's sake, get it!"*

*"I can't. It's too far, Jenny."*

*"Get it, Bill...damn it Bill, get it!"*

"With that thrust and near miss, the coats sank below the mud and now the black-dyed water was beginning to creep up my sides. Hell, the wet clothes even made me heavier than before. I was giving out, Doc, and because of the frigid mud I too was giving off vapor from my body.

"Again the sheep were crying even more, and the whole cold gruesome event was as if hell had decided a cold death was worse than burning alive. They were continually baying for life now...the noise for existence was beyond what a mind wanted to hear.

*"Get the baby, Bill!"*

*"God damn it! I'm going down, Jenny."*

*"Get it, damn you."*

*"Just hold my fucking legs, Jenny! I'm going down, damn you."*

"I was completely wet and shaking from the frigid mixture

of umber slush that was enveloping me. Even my breathing caused a motion and I knew I was sinking. One more chance was all I had, and so I took a breath as deep as my lungs could hold and thrust out with a splash. Suddenly I had hold of some gooey fur and the creature again struggled, which made me in turn go down up to my chin.

*"Pull, Jenny. Pull!"*

"Damn, I was going deeper, Doc, and was going to let go of the baby, when suddenly I felt as if Jenny had the strength of a tractor. Hell, that woman was grunting and crying at the same time, but I was sliding out. Yet with every pull I went deeper, and the mud-kicking lamb was still thrashing to save itself. Its head went under and then mine, but I felt the dragging and raised my head above the mire. The small black thing also came up, and Jenny was screaming as if that would intensify the lamb's will to give its maximum effort. I felt another release from the mud.

*"Pull, Jenny...pull!"*

"Then the water trap let go. I was now on some kind of stronger earth, and I in turn yanked the now unmoving lamb onto the pool's edge. Jenny was lying on the ground heaving and exhaling for more breath. A sudden kick from the youngster revived me as I held onto its fur for dear life. It was alive, and like Jenny lying next to me, the baby lamb was completely spent from the ordeal. Again I looked at the pool. The mother was now up to her head and was drawing in deep breaths. It was as if she had seen her child rescued and with that deliverance she now seemed calm, as if all was now well with her. Jenny rolled over to her side.

*"Help her, Bill!"*
*"I can't, Jenny. I can't get there."*
*"Oh my God."*

"I moved to her side and with a muddy hand placed her head on my wet and filthy covered shoulder to hide her eyes. She wasn't crying, Doc. It was more like emotional heaves.

*"Save her, Bill....please."*

*"I can't, Jenny."*

"I was utterly spent but turned and watched the whole cycle as another desperate wail came from the mother sheep.

*"I can't stand it...I can't stand it!"*

"She turned her head away and I kept her head tight into my wet shoulder. The next cry from the doomed animal seemed to be the loudest, and then with one last effort for freedom she moved her head higher. Then she went under.

*"Dear God, dear God,"* Jenny was repeating it over and over.

"Suddenly there came another splash and just the top part of the sheep's mouth emerged from the swirling chocolate mush. A last bay for mercy was almost a shriek, and again the animal disappeared.

"Almost as if on cue, two overhead floating crows gave a squawking and cruel farewell. Then total silence, and a pungent earthen breeze swept over us. We were nothing but a mixed matching clump of mud and slime cuddled next to the deadly pool. Under my other arm was the small, dingy-furred creature with overly white wide eyes as if searching for its parent. It was shaking and breathing in quick repetition.

*"It's done, Jenny."*

"I released my hold on her and she looked at the pool, her face was as black as a coal miner's, just as I knew mine was too.

*"God damn God. He's a monster."*

"Doc, we helped each other up after about five minutes and I carried the small sheep in my arms. With our drenching clothes everything became cold, and now I was worried if we had the ability to even make it back to the inn. Soaked through and with no coats, I can tell you, Doc, it took a toll on us and we both fell once or twice. But what seemed so unreal was that we barely said anything. Maybe our inner survival instinct knew we needed even that strength to keep going. When we did stop, the sheep would begin to bellow. We both knew it was wanting its mother's protection and not ours.

"After almost two hours we stumbled into the tavern. Jenny collapsed on the floor and I hung on the bar rail for support. My knee was killing me. Mr. and Mrs. Saunders both came running into the bar to help us. I recall Mr. Saunders had a problem making me let go of the lamb. Hell, I guess I was in as much shock as Jenny. But we made it, Doc, and I had had my first experience of death on the moors. It had all the sickening horror that Sir Arthur Conan Doyle had promised."

# Chapter 6

"I remember the next day that my limbs and knee were so sore, but I made it down to breakfast and had just related the whole event to the Saunders when the reverend came down.

*"How is she, Reverend?"*

*"Surprisingly well for such an adventure, but it could have been deadly you know, Mr. Hughes. It could have turned out rather nasty."*

"Somehow I was catching a hint that I was the cause of the whole experience.

*"Yes, it was a nightmare all right, but a life was saved because of your wife, Reverend. Not a soul, at least as you see it, but nevertheless a life."*

*"Yes, well I am still concerned about her going back out. I think perhaps it would be better if we stayed in Exeter. I called the local doctor last night and he gave her something, so she should be better now. Oh Mrs. Saunders, do see that she has a nice warm breakfast, if you please. I'd like for her to take it in our room and for her to rest all day."*

*"Yes, sir."*

*"I don't think she needs to venture out there anymore. Don't you agree, Mr. Hughes?"*

"Now I became 'Mr. Hughes' and not 'Bill.' I nodded in agreement, Doc. I just wanted him to go away.

*"Hmm. Guess I'll have to buy her a new coat today while in town also. Good day, Mrs. Saunders."*

*"Good day, Reverend, and I'll be checking on her all day, sir."*

*"Very kind."*

"He never acknowledged me, quickly slid on his coat, and slammed the door. As he left, I watched him get into his car and he looked back at me through the window. We were no longer friends.

*"I think he's extremely concerned, Mrs. Saunders."*

*"Yes, I could see that, Mr. Hughes, and I have a mind that he's not especially pleased with you."*

*"Yes, I rather noted that."*

*"Never you mind, Mr. Hughes. We know what you did and that little baby lamb is in the best of care. One of the farmers took it this morning and he said it was nothing short of a miracle that you and Mrs. Williamson saved it. I know he's a pastor and all that, but I personally think he's a little unpleasant. Oh, here I am again talking about our guest— shouldn't do that you know. My husband really gets upset with me on that account. Is there anything else, Mr. Hughes?"*

"It began to drizzle later in the morning so I stayed around the inn just to get the warmth back into my bones. I wrote about the lamb story most of the day as I knew it would make for a good article when I got back home. Jenny never came down, and while I was dining that evening I saw Mrs. Saunders carry a tray up the stairs. The piano stood alone and mute. Later that night at the bar some of the local farmers bought me some draughts and I was officially in good standing, even if I was a Yank. Unexpectedly, Mr. Saunders was kind enough to lend me one of his heavy coats for the remainder of my visit.

"Well, anyway, the next day I got up and looked out the window as I heard a door slam from outside. The reverend was just getting into his car, and the way it was parked I couldn't tell if Jenny was with him as he drove off toward Exeter. Quickly dressing, I went down and waited for what seemed like forever for Mrs. Saunders to come in the dining room for my breakfast order.

*"Good morning Mr. Hughes! Are you feeling better?"*

*"Yes, much better thank you."* But every bone and muscle ached.

*"Going to be a lovely day I think. How about a hot coffee and some ham and eggs? See, I know what you Americans have to start the day."*

*"Yes, that would be wonderful. Did the Williamsons leave this morning by chance?"*

*"Oh, the reverend? Yes, he just left, but the missus hasn't come down yet. He checked out this morning and is picking her up around lunchtime. The poor dear needs to be back home. I took some tea to her this morning but she seemed a bit down, if you know what I mean. I don't think the reverend approved of her taking such an awful chance on the moor for the poor sheep, you see."*

*"Yes."*

*"Well, I'll be right back with your coffee."*

*"Thank you, Mrs. Saunders."*

"Again I stared at the piano.

"After recharging myself with hot coffee and what seemed like an endless breakfast, I went back up for my sweater and coat. It was just a quick glimpse out my bedroom window, but I saw a figure cross the road. Damn, Doc, it was Jenny. She turned, looked back and forth down the road and then toward the inn for a moment. She caught sight of me at the window. I tried the window but it wouldn't budge, so I tapped and mouthed the words, 'Wait for me!'

"Doc, she gave me the most beautiful smile that ever came from a woman's face. It was her eyes and lips that came crashing into my chest—she was just so perfect. Then she turned and crossed the road and went straight for the main path that most of the visitors took to view the moor. I couldn't put the heavy jacket on fast enough. Hoping not to arouse too much attention by using the front staircase as other customers were eating in the dining room, I went thundering down the back steps. Doc, I had to see her. No matter what, I had to meet up with her.

"When I opened the heavy back door, morning chill greeted me, and as I rounded the building's corner I found the road was empty. I quickly made for the pathway and strolled along the trail for a while, but I simply couldn't see her. There were other paths that meandered off the main track, so I climbed the tallest rock I could find without going too far into the moor. Nothing. There was absolutely nothing. I decided just to stick to the main path.

"It must have easily been an hour or more that I found myself going farther into the heath. It was menacingly empty and deathly quiet except for an occasional gust of wind. I was reliving the *Wuthering Heights* novel in a world of romanticism—Jenny was my Cathy and I was Heathcliff. I kept seeing her hair floating over her in the wind. I heard her playing the piano. *Where was she?* Finally some unknown bird sounds broke the hush. Still there was no sign of her. But suddenly I saw a figure coming toward me from a higher elevation. It wasn't her; Jenny had a blue coat on and this person was in a deep red jacket. Funny how one can think back and recall colors, Doc."

"Yes, it is."

"Well, I decided to stop and lean against a rock. Meanwhile the red-coated person became a man.

*"Hello, lovely morning!"*

"He was the man who had the other hotel room. I had seen him eat and read by himself in the attached pub. He had kept strictly to himself during my stay and was in his late sixties or maybe in the first stages of seventy.

*"Yes, much better than yesterday by far."*

*"You're Mr. Hughes, aren't you?"*

*"Yes."*

*"I asked about you and the proprietor said you were a Baskerville enthusiast and lecturing at one of the colleges. Also that you write on the subject."*

*"Yes. I'm a retired policeman from New York, and it helps pass the time and brings in some much-needed income."*

*"Yes, I can well understand the income part. I'm a retired barrister, but you Americans call us lawyers 'sharks' or something like that."*

"I laughed at that.

*"You're right about that, Mr.—?"*

*"Wilfred Cabell."*

*"Cabell?"*

*"Struck you did it, Mr. Hughes?"*

*"God, yes. Are you any relation to the Squire Richard Cabell? You know, the one that somewhat helped foster the hound legend."*

*"I think so—since leaving my practice a year ago I have been investigating the old bones, and I believe I'm in the family line. Can't help feeling like a bit of a snack for the dog, you know. I'm too skinny I think in regards to a full meal for the beast, however."*

"This guy was all right...and I liked him, Doc.

*"Have you checked anything out?"*

*"Oh yes. Actually I think most of us come from the northern moor called Exmoor. Have you heard of it?"*

*"Yes. It's about twenty or thirty miles north of here I believe."*

64

*"Well, I'm not sure about American miles, but that's good enough."*

*"Have you found anything down here by chance?"*

*"Indeed. I stay here at the inn because it's centrally located and I can visit the surrounding moor town churches for baptismal and death records, you see. So far I have been lucky I guess."*

*"Really?"*

*"Some histories put the old squire at a place called Brook Manor over in the Buckfastleigh community. It's southeast of here on the edge of the moor. Still others say it was other places, but all are wrong. You see they don't go back to the sixteenth century. But the Buckfastleigh church had some Cabells there in their books, and indeed there was a Richard; however it didn't mention that he was a squire. His parents were of connected royal gentry, and strangely enough there is no record of his death or burial. That part I find interesting, don't you, Mr. Hughes? But again I have one of those genealogists looking for me and he thinks he's onto the squire."*

*"What about the other townships?"*

*"Nothing much so far though I'm only halfway around the moor towns, mind you—but it looks like if there was a Cabell scoundrel, he was here around Dartmoor. I mean the family line died out after his demise. Up north at Exmoor they are still thriving, and even more interesting, there aren't any squires recorded. Here it seems like he was obliterated off the records, but I am surmising again as an old attorney would do."*

*"Really good stuff for future studies, Mr. Cabell. You are a diamond in this bleak place."*

"Suddenly, Doc, Jenny just zoomed into my mind.

"Oh, by the way, did you see a woman on the path in your morning walk by any chance?"

"Oh, you mean Mrs. Williamson. Yes, yes, she was down near the bottom of that hill—see way over there. Kind of dangerous over in that part; really treacherous, sucking mud. I warned her to stick to the pathway. She's a lovely thing, but she seemed upset about something. Actually I think she might have been crying."

"Crying?"

"Yes. One can sense those things, can't we? You know...she was flushed. Probably had a row with the parson. But she thanked me and carried on. Was that you a few days ago with her on the rock, Mr. Hughes?"

"Yes it was. Then that had to have been you we saw almost lost in the cold haze? We spotted you over on that far hill. Do you by chance have a pet dog with you, Mr. Cabell?"

"No. Why do you ask?"

"We both saw something that was almost impossible to recognize. It was either a small pony or a black or dirty sheep just below the hill. It was headed in your direction—no, it was more like following you."

"Dear God, man, you're scaring me."

"Oh, I didn't mean to imply that—"

"Well, imply you did, and good for it, sir. I thought I was going daft. I couldn't shake the damn feeling that I was being followed. You know the old primeval instinct. It was inside of me that something was wrong. I kept looking around and stopping, but confound it, nothing showed itself. I was wondering if all this folklore was getting to me. Now that you and Mrs. Williamson saw something, well I'm colder than I was yesterday. I thought I was dreaming all *that night and put it aside, so this morning I ventured out to see if it was real or just my psyche working me over. But today I felt nothing—absolutely nothing. Now I am quite baffled, to be honest."*

"He stopped a few seconds and looked toward the horizon.

*"I best not think about it or I'll be called an old fool for sure. I often wondered what it would be like to stroll out there at night—you know, for the effect. However, I think I'll just stick to the family investigations. Besides, if I told my daughters this they would put me away."*

*"Yes, I see. But we did see that animal, Mr. Cabell. I'm not joking. Where in the hell is Mrs. Williamson? It's been more than two hours. I'm getting a little nervous."*

*"Oh, she'll be all right, I'm sure there are other hikers about the moor. She's a head on her shoulders, as far as I can tell."*

*"I think I'll go along the path some more if you don't mind."*

*"Of course, Mr. Hughes. Please let me know, won't you? But I'm sure she'll be around for tea shortly. See you at lunch?"*

*"Yes, I'll be there, Mr. Cabell."*

"Doc, I watched him head back up the rutted trail and back toward the warm inn, but I continued on for what was another hour. I even found myself calling her name from atop the rocks. But the vastness of the empty place just seemed to muffle my yells. It was as if the moor absorbed my voice into a soundless chamber. It just dropped away into a whisper. I was worried. And then those damned ravens began showing up making that cracking sound. They circled over me. I could hear them loud and clear, but my shouts went nowhere."

# Chapter 7

"Let's pause for a moment, Mr. Hughes, and you can go refresh yourself. The restroom is just over there. Then sit down again when you're ready and we'll resume where you left off."

"I think I will, Doc."

Bill made himself comfortable again after the required break.

"Now begin where you were trying to find the lady."

"I guess I stayed there till maybe two o'clock taking one path then another. I kept yelling, but there was nothing. I remember I was hungry but I was really worried for Jenny. Then I thought, *How stupid. Maybe she found another route back to the road.* Well, when I got back to the inn there was a cop car there, and as I entered I was immediately approach by Reverend Williamson.

*"Have you seen her, Mr. Hughes? Mr. Cabell said he met you on the moor and you seemed concerned for Jenny. Did you see her? Mr. Cabell believed she was upset."*

*"No, Carl, I didn't see her except for a few moments when I looked out the window this morning. She was headed down the path toward Fox Tor. I was also apprehensive when Mr. Cabell said he saw her way too far out there, so I tried calling and even took various trails. I just don't know, and it's getting damn cold. Can I get near the fire and maybe get something to drink?"*

"I looked out the window, Doc, and the gloom of the afternoon had begun to veil the landscape.

*"God—where could she be?"* The reverend was

trying to light a shaky cigarette.

*"She'll be along, old man, just wait a bit longer,"* Mr. Cabell tried to give the pastor some comforting advice.

*"I don't like this, Mr. Williamson,"* said the uniformed Constable Clayton who was standing near the fire with me. *"I think I had better call the boys and get some chaps to fan out along the paths. It'll be getting dark soon and damned dangerous out there. We'll get the helicopter up, sir, but the mist is settling in so we had better get kicking. Don't fret, sir. We'll find the missus."*

"It went on all night, Doc. More police from the surrounding towns came in. Some brought motorized bikes and the helicopter zoomed overhead beaming what was like a warm glow in a cold glaze. Scent dogs were heard barking in the background. I was worn out, Doc. I would have gone too, but all I could do was stay there in the pub as volunteers came in and out to warm up. The reverend was constantly on the phone, but still no news was forthcoming. You know, I started to feel down, Doc—maybe it was the police instinct. Inside me I knew no news was coming that night."

"Yes, go on."

"Well, by one or two o'clock in the morning the call to stop the search was given and the poor fellows came in wet, muddy, and just exhausted. Constable Clayton thanked them all and said to go get some rest and they would resume the search at seven in the morning. I was scared for Jenny and I thought for a moment that I would go on the hunt by myself. I missed her, Doc. I was hurting for her smile and everything about her in the worst way. I even went over to the piano and plunked a few keys, then whispered to myself for her to come back to me."

"That's understandable."

"I finally turned in, but really didn't sleep. I kept thinking of her out there—even worse, maybe she was screaming for help and unable to move in a mud bog. It was going deeper and deeper inside me; it was tearing me up. I grabbed two stiff gulps of scotch off the bed table and then left the world as a searchlight struck my window panes from a helicopter that roared overhead."

"You're sitting straight up, Bill. Sit back and be comfortable."

"The next day I was introduced to Jenny's parents who had flown in from vacationing in Spain. They seemed more at ease than me or the reverend, and I wondered how could they could control their emotions. All the next day search parties were scattered across the area, and another chopper came in. No news came back. By then the reverend's relatives were also there and he was a mess. Blaming himself—you know how it is. Finally they took him away, but the headquarters for the hunt was made at the inn. I felt useless, Doc, so I put on a couple of sweaters, walking boots, and Mr. Saunders' borrowed coat and headed out.

"I decided to take the paths that were behind the inn. Maybe she had crossed the road unseen and took the more unused paths. As I went deeper into the moor, every so often I would find myself calling her name, but only the ravens answered me. In the distance I could make out a chopper and sometimes hear the clapping of its propellers. Stupidly I still went on and even lost sight of the inn after climbing some rather large hills; then the damn path became smaller and split into two directions. Still I never stopped yelling for her. And then the trail became almost no longer discernible, so I tried to keep some kind of recognizable view in order to have a point of origin to fall back on. The ground became mush, Doc, and the idea of the notorious man- and animal-sucking bog hit home. I almost went into a panic as the whole event with Jenny and the sheep sent me into a coward's shiver.

"When I rounded a small, stone-clustered hill, I thought I saw something. It was one of those wild ponies I heard about and it quickly bolted and disappeared over a small rise in the terrain. I'm not sure if I was just so scared of finding myself being sucked into a bog or just being lost in the dark, but I turned back. Doc, I wanted to be the one to rescue her so badly...I wanted her back. I felt so depressed. You see, I had let her down. She was waiting for me to rescue her and I had been unable to save her, just as I failed the mother sheep. They say, Doc, that as we get older we're unable to control our emotions. Well, I wanted to cry out in frustration as I made my way back to the inn. The steel-colored, grim mist just made it worse.

"That night brought on a heavy rain and wind. The television was alive with Jenny being reported missing and insights of her as the faithful minister's wife. I just watched it from the pub stool, Doc. Every once in a while a cold chill ran through every fiber of my body. Even my muscles were hurting. But through all that, Doc, I knew I had not done enough for her. I think she wanted me to help her and I didn't."

"No way, Bill. Jenny, to be truthful, had been lost way before you came in."

"But I could have—"

"You could have done nothing, Bill. You were but a moment in a long string of underlying disappointments for the girl. She was on a path that was hers alone. But did she ever turn up?"

"The next day I went back out again. Hell, I was driven, Doc. I was driven to find her. At first I felt the policeman instinct to be of help, but once more I knew it was more than that—I wanted to have her for myself. It was really as simple as that, Doc. The reverend didn't deserve her; I did. If I could find her I knew she would in some fantastic way realize that she would belong to me. Once more a helicopter whipped overhead as I trudged down the back path again, but now I could recognize the mud bogs ahead. The danger didn't seem to matter. If she could have lasted through the

71

two nights and the chill, though no doubt life-draining, she could still be alive. But as I said before, I knew she had a fortitude in her even though she was so totally desperate. While I headed this time to a huge tor hill that looked almost ten miles away, I was in denial that she would walk to her death—I couldn't think like that.

"As I neared the top of a rocky crag, after walking for what seemed like hours, I was worn out. I began calling her name, and just as I rounded an enormous boulder, I found myself in front of an opening where a mammoth granite slab was leaning against another the same size. But instead of it being a natural entrance, it was more of a manmade cave. Suddenly I realized that I stood in front of one of those ancient copper mines that I had read about and that were also mentioned in Conan Doyle's story. I could even tell where manmade strike marks were still identifiable along the entryway.

"As I stared in the hole I saw it became pitch black after only a few yards, and even a draft of freshened air from within slapped my face. I called out Jenny's name. Nothing came back. *But what if she was too weak or unconscious to return my yell?* I thought. I was afraid, Doc. The dark alleyways of the city I understood, but this was not my terrain, and the episode of the previous mire and sheep incident made me even more hesitant. Again I made more attempts at calling into the dark void. Nothing, absolutely nothing came back, not even an echo. I crept in farther and was terrified I would slip into a shaft or something, so after the reflected light against the rock walls no longer gave me any vision whatsoever, I lit my lighter. Again and again I called for Jenny.

"Then, just as I was about to turn around back toward the entrance, I saw something whitish on the crushed stone ahead. I went in deeper. The lighter went out and I almost panicked, but thankfully it flicked on again."

"What was it you found?"

"It was just a small piece of soiled cloth, no bigger than a few inches. Again I called out for her. But then, Doc, that's when my heart fell to my feet. A noise came from somewhere."

"What kind of noise?"

"It was like a loud low moan, but deep. I can't explain the sound, but I was frozen and I felt my eyes intensely try to see into the darkness beyond the fire from the lighter. I remember distinctly that I knew it was not Jenny, and no matter if my imagination was running out of bounds I was getting out of there fast. Hell, I was scared, Doc."

"Go on."

"As I made my way back to the entrance, I never heard the sound again and was really hoping to God I wouldn't. When I caught the first glimpse of light from the cave opening I felt a tinge of safety, but all the while I was noting where I stepped. Once again I looked up for comfort from the entrance glow when I suddenly froze with stark terrifying fear—something had crossed in front of the cave mouth and momentarily blocked out my saving beacon of daylight. Doc, I couldn't move. *What the hell was it?* I called out, 'Who's there?' Only the entrance breeze was barely audible. I shouted for Jenny too, but once more only a whistle of wind returned my shaky cry. I continued to move forward and enough reflected glow allowed me to extinguish my lighter. Finally, I was out. I looked in every direction and again yelled to see if anyone was around. I was alone."

"And you saw nothing?"

"Absolutely nothing. All I can recall is that I wanted away from there—and fast. Both my mind and heart were thumping. Over and over I kept saying to myself, *What the hell happened? What was that shadow? What was that sound?* I certainly wasn't dreaming. That something had to have been big to block out the light at the cave entrance. I can tell you, Doc, I made it back to the hotel twice as fast as I took to get to that tor."

"Did you report what happened to the constable?"

"Yes, and they sent out three guys to check out the cave, but they only came back with the small piece of cloth that I had found and dropped when I had the crap scared out of me."

"Keep going."

"Well, after two days the volunteers were exhausted. Then the police contingent dispersed after another day. The helicopters even stopped hovering over the hills by the fourth day. I watched how Jenny's parents thanked all those involved in the search efforts with humble gratitude and even came over to offer their appreciation for my involvement."

"So she was never found, not even the body?"

"No. She vanished. The damned moor took her, and I still hurt for her. Right here in this stupid pitiful heart. I loved her, Doc— and don't give me that psychiatry junk about reasons why it happened so fast—all I know was that I was in love with her. I realized it was more than sex, Doc; she had hold of me…I wanted to own her, to care for her and have her all to myself. God, it hurt so bad to know I could not be with her."

"Okay, Bill, go on."

"I called the school and even that place was in chaos. Apparently with the electrical power failure, the pipes in the restrooms and some living quarters in the school had frozen and burst. My chief advisor said it was a mess and that I might think of returning home or taking an extended vacation until everything was up and running. I counted my money and chose the latter. Thank God it was off season and the inn was in nowhere land for catching any tourists. There were empty rooms. I explained my dilemma to the Saunders and they even cut the rate. They were just plain old good people, Doc."

"Let's get back to where we were if we can."

"Okay. I bicycled over to Princetown, which is basically the next borough. I wanted to see where Conan Doyle stayed and began the Baskerville story. But Jenny was always on my mind."

"Yes, I understand."

"Princetown was a small place but neat as a pin and the weather had turned warmer. But you know, as I rode home and looked over that moor, I remember the clouds showing dots of light on the surfaces of the ruddy brown hills. And she came into my mind. Where was she? Maybe she wanted to play dead and just start over again with nothing. I wanted to believe that real bad—she couldn't be out there so alone."

"Let's move on if we can—past Jenny, Bill. We need to see what caused these nightmares."

"You're right, Doc. It was on the last day that the copters flew over that the small rock-and-roll production company arrived. They had accommodations in Exeter but were filming in Postbridge. I watched them set up just down an old, worn road near a granite cluster. Lord, the music blared out from a recording through two huge loudspeakers. The kid star was jumping from one rock to another all the time just mouthing the words. The horrible banging went on all day, and when Mr. Cabell arrived back from one of his town visits he went directly in and complained to the Saunders about the noise. But it was over in the afternoon and the crew started to pack up. I think that was the evening Cabell and I dined together—yes that was it, because that was the night it all really began..."

# Chapter 8

"…it all really began. It..."

"Now relax, easy does it. Just take a deep breath…exhale. Go slow."

"A few of the local farmers were in the pub and we could hear them as we ate in the small dining room. Then the door swung open and in paraded the movie crew, the kid, this knockout girl who was his mate, and lastly his parents. They were loud and I could tell Mr. Cabell did not approve. They asked Mr. Saunders if they could use the bar television VCR so they could look at the recording while the draft beer was being passed around the bar.

"When the tape began, they burst out laughing and pointing at the kid dancing around on the screen. God, it was awful. Over and over they played the act—then it happened. One of the guys said something.

*"Wait a minute! Run that back. No, farther…Now start it again. What the hell is that in there? Did any of you notice it before?"*

"The others became quiet and Cabell and I both wondered what brought the frivolity to an abrupt halt. We listened more intently.

*"What the hell? Look back there, over at the big ledge back there near the top of the hill in background. Damn, Roddy, run it back again."*

"Cabell and I stood up and looked toward the screen.

*"Now run it in slow mode this time, Roddy."*

*"There. See it, boys? By God, it's—it's a cat—a huge black cat."*

*"Shit! I believe he's right,"* another stated.

*"Don't be daft. It's a sheep, you idiots."*

*"Run it back again, Roddy."*

"We came closer to the others and the farmers were now amongst us.

*"It's no sheep and certainly no pony. What the hell is it?"*

*"It's a sheep."*

*"Brian, I worked on one of those rug farms for five years and I know sheep when I see 'em—and that ain't no sheep."*

*"It's the light against the sheep that makes it look like it's black."*

*"No way—it's hunched."*

*"Big, ain't it?"*

"Then the kid came on.

*"I've got it—we'll use it in the film. It was given to us! The Baskerville Hound!"*

*"Yeah, it'll work all right. The news will eat it up."*

*"Come on now, boys, let's get out of here. This place is dead. Let's do some real celebrating in Exeter. We just made a bundle with that shot—a real bundle."*

"The crowd was so noisy as they left, Doc. I recall hearing the engines starting and the gravel grinding as they raced out to the road. But the pub was back at peace again. Mr. Cabell had disappeared, and the farmers took up the conversation.

*"Now there you go, boys. We finally know what's been chewing on the wild sheep in the area and making those God-awful wails."*

*"I thought Constable Clayton popped those dogs?"*

"So he says, the lazy bastard. Well, he missed this one. Hell, he's blind anyway so what makes you think he got any of them?"

"I can say one thing for sure, that was the biggest damn dog or cat I've ever seen about these parts. Maybe the Baskerville junk ain't no tall tale after all."

"Ah, stuff it...it was a sheep in the picture."

"But how can Robert Burnhill's cow be attacked and chewed up by only one dog?"

"Twern't one dog—where there's one, there's more. Clayton just ain't got any of them as far I can see."

"Maybe you're right, Sidney. Remember a few weeks back that horse they found? Hell, he was mangled...there were pieces of him found all over the place."

"Aye, true enough. I'm turning in a complaint to district. Clayton ain't doing nothin' and the park people just cut the road grass. Damn, we need help. Who knows, this pack of dogs could get at the children about the area."

"Yeah, especially if they're that big. Never seen anything like it."

"I tell ya, it was a filthy dirty sheep."

"Sheep, my ass."

"Lordy! Look at the time—my missus is gonna do me in for sure, and that howling is getting on her nerves in the worst way."

"Yeah, we heard it near our house two nights ago. Maybe we need to go after the dog pack if Constable Clayton can't do the job."

"Gotta go, boys. Drink up."

"I'm behind ya."

"Then with the door slamming behind the last customers,

Mr. Saunders and I just stared at each other. Again the gravel crunched and pinged as the vehicles left the lot. The hotel owner clicked the television off and turned on some music, and it all mingled with clinking sounds of the glasses being washed behind the bar.

*"A wild night, Mr. Hughes."*

*"I'll say. Where did Mr. Cabell go?"*

*"Oh, I saw him slip upstairs."*

*"Well, that's where I'm headed too."*

"No sooner, Doc, had I said good night than another car arrived. The door came open and Officer Clayton came in rubbing his hands.

*"Downright chilly. Any tea? Oh, good evening, Mr. Hughes. Hope all is well?"*

*"Okay with me, but I'm afraid you're in for it."*

*"Whatever do you mean?"*

*"Tell him, Saunders."*

*"John, you know Sidney Johnson, old man Ferguson, and Morse Hudson? They have the farms within shouting distance of each other."*

*"Why sure—good boys. Work hard on their farms."*

*"They saw a video that those music boys made today, and somehow they caught on film what they thought was a dog in the picture—and a dammed big one at that— standing on a ledge in the film. It was way in the distance."*

*"Are you sure it was a dog and not a deer or pony in the video?"*

*"Not really, but our lads were guessing it was."*

*"What did they say?"*

*"That you claimed you had popped all the wild dogs about, but you let the biggest one get away, and maybe you didn't get any of them."*

*"Hell I didn't! Oh, I know there may be a few still around, but no more packs. I got them."*

*"Well, they're not drinking on that, and the howling near their farms has them edgy. The wives are giving them grief, John."*

*"Damn it, every time I get the call I head straight out, but when I arrive there's nothing there."*

*"You might get ready for some tongue-lashing because they're plenty sore after seeing the film, I can tell you that. Right, Mr. Hughes?"*

*"I guess so. Of course, as an ex-policeman I'm on the constable's side. All there seems to be in a lawman's life is 'just a few minutes earlier' and we would have got the culprit."*

*"Right you are, Mr. Hughes. How about that tea? I'll go see the boys tomorrow and get the thing settled, besides—"*

"I was just ready to head upstairs, Doc, when Clayton's walkie-talkie crackled and interrupted his conversation. It was a complaint about a dog barking at the Johnson farm.

*"Damn it!"*

*"Well, there you go now,"* said Saunders.

*"Care to chase the Dartmoor hound, Mr. Hughes? It's against rules, but we're badge brothers and all that stuff. A night on the moors, huh?"*

*"Aye...be good for your stories, Mr. Hughes,"* said the hotel owner.

*"Okay, I'll give it a try."*

"I pulled the parka around me and somehow got in what I think was a car. It was so small, Doc, that my legs were in my throat. I think they call it a mini something or other. So there I was tooling down a dark Dartmoor moor road.

*"Where's the Johnson farm?"*

*"Near Ponsworthy. It's about fifteen or twenty minutes."*

"As we drove down the road, the stars were as I had never seen them before, billions of them. The dark gloom of the late night made those things look like spotlights. It was just plain inky black as black could be, Doc. But there were also pockets of mist that wrapped around us as we rumbled along, and I couldn't help wondering about Jenny too. Over and over I asked myself, *Where is she?"*

"That's all right. You were just feeling your emotions, Bill. Nothing wrong there. Go on."

" *"We're just about there now, Mr. Hughes."*

*"Call me, Bill. Hell, like you said, we're partners now."*

"Imagine this, Doc—me with an English Bobby partner. Just before we crested a hill Clayton cut off the lights, and then as we topped the bluff he cut the engine. He rolled down his window and the cold completely absorbed the car's heat. Our breaths were a hazy smoke.

*"Hear anything, Bill?"*

*"Nothing."*

*"There! Listen!"*

*"I hear it."*

*"It's just over by that tor."*

*"What the hell is a tor anyway?"*

*"It's nothing. Just means a granite spire or a clump of moor rocks. It's an old Welsh or English term."*

*"There it is again, hear it?"*

*"Yeah."*

"Clayton didn't start the car but shifted and let the vehicle coast down the hill and stopped. Without thinking I suddenly blurted out a command.

*"Don't open that door!"*

*"What?"*

*"Unscrew the dome light."*

*"Damn, Bill, you'd make a bloody good partner. Now give me that rifle on the backseat."*

"It was a small rifle, Doc, and he fed it from a box of bullets he kept in the glove compartment.

*"I'm not supposed to be doing this without permission—but out here it's a constant mission without permission, if you get what I mean."*

*"Don't worry. I follow the street code."*

*"Good man, let's go."*

"We eased out of the car without slamming the doors and I followed him down a small ravine. Again we heard the howl, only this time it was abruptly cut off. Then came the sound of a broken bottle against the stone. A soft glow illuminated the granite boulders. As we turned the corner he had the gun at point.

*"All right, fun's over."*

"A small group let out a shocked yell.

*"Wait Officer, don't shoot!"*

"Standing before us were three teenage boys and two girls. A small battery lamp was the glow and sitting next to it an enormous black box. Clayton lowered the weapon and we both walked toward the shaking kids.

*"A flippin' tape recorder, all the time a flippin' tape recorder. Who's the leader of this social club?"*

"The frightened teens, all at the same time, looked at the tallest boy.

*"Officer, it was just a fun thing. We were just having some fun. We didn't mean any harm, honest. I mean..."*

*"Well, you can be quiet and let me see your*

*identification please.*"

"The poor kid's hand was shaking so that he had a hell of a time getting the card out of his wallet. Memories, Doc—it brought back a million memories of street working here in the city."

"Go on, Bill."

"*"Please Officer, we'll leave right this instant. Can't you give us a chance? Please?"* the others pleaded behind him.

*"Do you realize the grief you have been giving the folks around here? Now you want me to let you go scot free with a pat on the ass?"*

"They were at his mercy, but I knew Clayton was just making them sweat a little.

*"Okay, get out of here—not you, son."*

"Then a girl spoke up.

*"But Officer, he has the car. It's just around those other rocks."*

*"Okay, here's the deal. Tomorrow all of you come back here and clear up every piece of broken glass. If I find so much as a splinter, I'll haul you in. I'm going to keep your ID, son, and this boom box. You come back and pick it up at the station. Be there at three o'clock—school or no school—or you're locked up. Got that?"*

*"Yes, Officer. Thank you, Officer."*

"I watched Clayton then write something on a small pad.

*"Here's the station address, and if the police stop you, give them this if they ask for your driver's license."*

*"Yes, Officer."*

*"Where do you go to school?"*

"They all voiced in chorus, *"Exeter."*

*"Okay, now get! And drive slow. And if I ever catch any of you out in this area again, you'll not forget the*

*consequences. Do I make myself clear on that point?"*

*"Yes, Officer."*

"Within two, maybe three seconds we were alone, Doc. Never seen such light-footed kids. We could hear their car roar off and shifting gears.

*"Damned teenagers. For months and months here I have been chasing kids. Should have made them run back to Exeter. Here, Bill, grab the light and I'll carry this big, damn boom box thing."*

"Then he abruptly halted.

*"Well, now here's a bit of luck, and it's near full."*

"Clayton, with the huge tape player under one arm, reached down and grabbed a bottle that lay near the light.

*"Bless me bones. Scotch!"*

"As we trudged back up the hill I heard Clayton take a swig or two. Then as we came near the top of the crest I threw the light on the car and quickly got in.

*"Want a bit of warmth, Bill?"*

"He handed me the bottle through the window. The liquid burned down my throat and it gave me a blessed searing heat. It was so cold out, Doc. I handed the bottle back to him and he took another deep gulp. I can remember that real well. God, it was dark, so I screwed the dome light back in. Clayton ejected the bullet from the rifle and it went flying into some brush.

*"Where the hell did that bullet go? Oh, to hell with it."*

"Next he stuck the rifle in the backseat, and all the while he was cussing away about the kids and the anguish they had caused. I rolled up the window, and then I heard him open the trunk to put the boom box inside. And then…and then..."

"You all right, Bill?"

"...and then, D-Doc…"

84

"You're shaking, Bill. Sit back down and take a deep breath. Now exhale."

"And then…and then…"

"Easy, son. You have tears coming, so if you want to cry, let it go—let it go."

"There…there was a roar that almost shook the car, Doc. It was so guttural, so deep and near me, Doc. It was so strong it deafened my ears—it bounced off the rocks and back into the car. I was so incredibly scared, Doc. Then I grabbed the window handle and rolled it down.

*"You lousy son of a bitch, Clayton. You scared the living crap out of me! Cut that God damn box thing off."*

"The trunk shut and he came around me window. I heard him drop the bottle.

*"You low down shit. You almost gave me a heart attack."*

*"Hand me the rifle, Bill."*

*"What?"*

*"Hand me the fucking rifle. I didn't do that."*

*"What?"*

*"God damn it, hand me the gun, Bill!"*

*"Come on Clayton, cut the crap."*

*"Give me the fucking bullets, damn you!"*

"My hands were shaking so bad, Doc, as I reached over the backseat and handed him the gun through the window. Next I opened the glove compartment and grabbed a half-opened box of bullets. I dropped some of them in the car as I gave them to him; then he spilled some as he tried to load the rifle. Seated as I was, I watched the front of his pants get wet. Then as he was frankly trying to get a bullet in the chamber, I turned and saw…I saw—"

"Now calm yourself, Bill."

"Dear God, I saw…"

"Easy Bill, sit back down. What did you see, son?"

"I-I saw it, D-Doc—I-I-I s-saw it!"

"Saw what, Bill? You're stuttering."

"I saw something red looking at me between the boulders on the driver's side. They were in a head, Doc. Oh Jesus, Doc, it was a…h-head with eyes! Those eyes, D-Doc…"

"Now stop, Bill. You're going to stop now. Get hold of yourself. I can't understand you if you're stuttering."

"Those eyes in that giant head, they were red, Doc, red as fire and coals."

"Here, drink this. Easy now, Bill, easy. Sip it. Sip it slowly."

"No, no—I got to go on!"

"You're getting overly excited, Bill."

"Everything that is vile and cruel—all the seething hate and unfathomable evil was looking at me. Doc, it was ripping my insides out and it was just looking at me! God, the whole black, four-legged thing was huge, and it yawned…its mouth—the teeth were not teeth but white knives. Oh Jesus! I can only remember that I was in such fear that my mouth was open and I couldn't do anything. I wanted to scream, Doc, but the only thing I could do was look at this demon. It was a demon—oh my God, those eyes!

"Then it let go another roar and I suddenly began kicking and wanting out of the car. I tried to open the door, but Clayton was crumpling to the ground and I was trapped. Clayton's body was not letting me out, Doc. I wanted out! I wanted out! Please Jesus, have mercy—I just wanted out. Oh Mother of God, it was coming to the driver's side of the window! It looked at me. I was dying, Doc—it was sucking the very soul out of me. My heart was wanting to—"

"Stop it, son."

"I was wanting to come out of my body, Doc. The thing wanted to stick its head in the window, but it was as if the head was too fucking big, Doc. It wouldn't fit through the window! Its mouth seemed to glow, not from its breath but just from some sort of foam or froth or something, I don't know, I don't know—oh my God!"

"Damn it, Bill, stop it now!"

"It was trying to get its head in, Doc—and all I could do was try to breathe and scream, and I started kicking everywhere—the dash, the door, and at the monstrous head. Oh those infernal eyes!! Oh, I...I..."

"Stop now. Just stop. Listen to me, Bill. Stop!"

# Chapter 9

"How long have I been asleep?

"About fifteen minutes."

"I was out of control. I never thought in all my years I'd lose it."

"You were just hysterical, but you're back now and calm. Here, put this on your head. It'll cool you down."

"I have to go on, Doc."

"Are you sure Bill?" We can do this tomorrow"

"No, I have to go on."

"Very well. I'll tell you when to stop… then you must."

"Okay."

"I remember suddenly waking up in the car."

"Are you sure you want to go on?"

"Yes, yes—I'm okay now. God, I'm soaking."

"Now calm down."

"I remember waking up in the car. I shot up like a rocket and started yelling again but finally stopped because I was just drained. My head was bursting. Clayton was lying facedown on the ground. It was so still, Doc. It was almost like outer space would be like. I mean nothingness, no night sounds, no wind. It was lifeless. I heard the constable moan and I opened the door, pushing him away, and grabbed the rifle and opened the chamber. It was still empty. I picked up a bullet off the ground and I loaded it. God, I was so terrified. My hands were like rubber. I kicked Clayton's side, never for an instant looking down. I just kept looking around.

*"Get up, damn you. Get up!"*

"He moaned again.

*"Get your ass up now!"*

"Doc, I was shaking so bad, and I was colder in the groin. When I finally looked down my pants were wet too. I was absolutely shattered—I lost everything. My mouth, Doc, was bone dry, but my hair was soaking and cold from the stark sweating terror of it all.

*"Get your butt up, Clayton. We've got to get out of here!"*

"Slowly he grabbed the door handle and pulled himself up and ran his fingers through his hair.

*"My God in heaven, what happened?"*

*"Just get in the car, Clayton."*

"He collapsed again, so I pushed him in my seat and went around to the driver's side, all the while holding that puny rifle to point. I was shaking so much, Doc, that I could hardly get the window rolled up and lock the doors. Clayton was moaning and lay sagging against the passenger door. I got the keys off his belt and started the thing and immediately put the lights on. There was nothing, Doc, nothing—just the blackness and a soft mist rolling in over the rocks. The engine turned over, and I smashed the rear bumper as I backed into a boulder—hell, the gears and steering are all turned around on those British cars. Finally, I lurched forward and spun the wheels till I was going as fast as the engine could go down that tiny country road. My mind was bursting. I wanted away. I saw things that the human mind is not supposed to see. I was…I was..."

"Now stop, Bill. Just stop. While you were out I had lunch sent up from the cafeteria downstairs. Just go wash your face. We're going to take a break."

----------- ----------- -----------

"Now. You'll feel better with something in your stomach, Bill."

"Thanks for the snack, Doc, but I have a knot in my stomach that won't quit."

"Just sit back now, sip the Coke, and rest. When you're ready, just start talking."

"I don't recall getting back to the inn. I was suddenly awakened with a knocking on a door. I raised myself up and discovered I was in my room with my damp clothes on and a blanket was thrown over me. It took me a minute to clear my senses. The knocking never seemed to stop.

*"Mr. Hughes, you all right, sir?"*

*"Yes, yes—I'm okay. Thank you, Mr. Saunders."*

"But I wasn't. I felt like I had been on one hell of a night bender. My head was throbbing.

*"Mr. Hughes, there are a couple of gentlemen that would like to see you."*

*"Gentlemen?"*

*"Yes, sir. They said they'll wait for you downstairs in the dining room."*

*"I can't make it now."*

*"It's the police, Mr. Hughes."*

*"The police?"*

*"Yes, sir."*

*"Okay, okay. I'll be down shortly."*

"I raised myself up and stumbled into the tiny bathroom. When I looked in the mirror I saw no one I knew. All my facial features looked like they were sagging from my skull, and my eyes were completely bloodshot and darkened. I looked as though I had been in a ten-round boxing match and definitely lost. After trying to wash up, I pretended that I was restored to some type of appearance and went downstairs.

*"Have a seat, Mr. Hughes. I'm Inspector George Martin and this is Sergeant Stanley Hopkins. Could we ask*

90

*what happened last night?"*

"God, Inspector, I don't know for sure."

"Come, come, Mr. Hughes. We know you're a retired officer—certainly you can help us if anyone can?"

"Ask Constable Clayton. I'm not sure I can—"

"We can't, Mr. Hughes. Seems he had some sort of a stroke and is now in hospital. He's in bad shape they tell me."

"Good God Almighty! Clayton out of it?"

"Yes, it would seem so."

"If I make a statement, can I go back to Cambridge? I'm exhausted."

"Oh, you can, sir—but we'll have to ask you to stay here a bit longer on our money until we get this mess straightened out, you see. Now can you help us? You drove the car back didn't you?"

"I think so. Yes, I...I did."

"Then let me bring you up to date, Mr. Hughes. You drove up to the inn last night lying on the horn continuously until you were dragged out by Mr. Saunders and—what's his name, Sergeant?"

"Mr. Cabell, sir."

"Oh yes, Mr. Cabell. They both got you upstairs. Then they carried Constable Clayton inside. Mrs. Saunders administered to him while they called the ambulance. And now we've got a man who's fighting for his life, a wrecked police car, and both of you smelling of spirits."

"Jesus."

"I don't want to question Him, Mr. Hughes, just you."

"All right, but you're not going believe this, Inspector—even I don't. I won't let myself believe it."

91

*"Try me, Mr. Hughes."*

"He was spit and polish, Doc. His suit fit him perfectly and his bald head only accented his walrus mustache. The youngster next to him was writing on a notepad, and the boy's clothes were like all up-and-coming detectives who graduated out of the uniform—cheap and ill-fitting. The threads are just too expensive."

"Take another sip. Take a breath...now that's better. Now go on, Bill."

"Well, Doc, I went through the whole scenario and they called Mr. Saunders in to verify Clayton and I leaving on the call. Mr. Cabell was standing near the door and he said that he was not sure what happened, but he knew me and I was a stout fellow. Cabell went so far as to defend me as a teacher and lecturer at Cambridge. My story had to have merit—or something like that—because when they heard that, I felt the inspector lose some of his firmness toward me.

*"Well, we know both of you didn't juice it up out there because Clayton's alcohol level was negligible. Maybe you were somewhat inebriated, Mr. Hughes?"*

*"He was not, Inspector. Both Mr. Saunders and I can vouch for that also,"* Cabell again came to my rescue.

*"Well, what about that dog you were rambling about when they brought you and Clayton inside?"*

*"I don't know. I almost went out of my mind, Inspector. It was massive, just like I told you—not like any dog on earth. I tell you it did have red eyes, damn it, I saw them...and those teeth... I think I saw something you're not supposed to see."*

*"Calm down, Mr. Hughes. I can promise that your nightmare was wrapped in Sherlock Holmes. Oh, I'm not saying there aren't any nice size, wild dogs out there, but that hound myth is a fable, sir—a fiction story. But as a*

*teacher you know all of this stuff. Maybe a dog did come at you—they're hungry and wild as the wind on the moors—but we'll see. Now would you mind if we drove out there to the spot together? You know, just to clear things up a bit?"*

*"Don't patronize me, Inspector Martin. I'm a cop, remember?"*

*"Yes, yes, forgive me. But that's why I want your help."*

*"I can't go out there anyway."*

*"Why?"*

*"I just can't. Besides I'm not sure where it was that we stopped."*

*"I believe it was near Mr. Johnson's farm, Mr. Hughes. Can't be that many roads in that wild area. Come on, let's have a go at it shall we?"*

"I tried to stand, Doc, but my legs were wobbly as they helped me to their car. All the while Cabell was scolding them that their actions were intolerable and I needed rest. But within minutes I was in the backseat bumping along the road. It was as bright a day as I had seen since arriving in England.

*"Now just tell us if anything looks familiar, Mr. Hughes."*

*"It was pitch black, Inspector, and all this is new to me. I don't recall any special features except for some pointed rocks."*

"We made turns, stopped a few places, but there was nothing I could recognize. It was finally when we turned down a dirt road and went to the top of a hill that I saw a small farm cottage with various outbuildings clustered near it. The inspector told his assistant to stop the car.

*"That's Johnson's farm, Mr. Hughes. We'll cruise down the hill a little."*

93

"The young sergeant quickly made the discovery.

*"Look, Inspector, deep tire ruts!"*

*"Good. We must be near the spot."*

"It was still all a blur to me, Doc. Daylight meant nothing; everything was mixed up.

*"Now, there's a nice granite assortment, Mr. Hughes."*

"We came to a halt and the sergeant, Hopkins, opened the door to let me out.

*"Let's get some air, shall we?"*

"The three of us advanced into the muddy circle that was bounded by some natural gray stone walls.

*"Don't get your feet wet, gents."*

*"Look Inspector, this is the spot! There's a bottle on the ground and near it some ammunition,"* the young policeman's voice seemed overjoyed.

*"Yes, and the boulder over to the right has a dink where you said the car struck. This is the place then, is it not, Mr. Hughes?"*

"I still only remembered the dark, Doc, but it had to be the site, and I acknowledged it with a nod.

*"I guess so, but I don't want to be here, Inspector."*

"I still recall that I started an uncontrollable quiver. The whole nightmare was returning.

*"Sergeant, go down around that boulder and see if that has any broken glass about it."*

"I watched as the young man made his way down the hill just as Clayton and I had done and disappeared behind the boulders. He reappeared with something sparkling in his had.

*"This is it all right, sir. Bits of glass everywhere."*

*"Good—then come on back up."*

*"Now the car was parked here, Mr. Hughes. Where*

*did you say this dog appeared that caused you trouble?"*

"I looked over to my left and pointed to an opening between two huge rocks.

*"It must have been there—I remember the crevice."*

*"Good, Mr. Hughes. Good. We'll have a look-see."*

"I stayed near the car and he carefully stepped over muddy tire tracks and went to the opening. I was now beginning to shake like I had a fever, Doc. I didn't want to be there.

*"Hmm. Yes, there are various marks of some kind, but they're not much of anything but holes. The mud has closed up anything distinguishing. What do you think, Mr. Hughes?"*

"As I went next to the inspector, the sergeant called him.

*"Want me to take the scotch bottle with us, sir?"*

*"Yes, Hopkins, we'll check it out—and pick up those rounds too."*

*"Right you are, sir."*

*"Well, Mr. Hughes, what do make of these?"*

*"Nothing but indentations now. What about behind the stone?"*

*"I'll check."*

"He came back shaking his head, Doc.

*"Same thing—just large holes."*

"As we drove back I was just wanting to get out of that place and go back to Cambridge—in fact, I wanted to come back home. I had enough of the place. First Jenny, now this. It was too much.

"When we returned to the inn the inspector excused himself and went to the restroom, and I was left with the young sergeant complaining about the inspector's new orders. The sergeant was to take charge of Clayton's duties. He was to pick up a car at Exeter, then patrol the district until a replacement could be found for the sick constable. As the inspector and sergeant headed out, I noticed Cabell

95

was in the pub with Saunders, along with three men with their backs to me at the bar. When they turned around I recognized it was the archeology group.

*"Now you sit down here, old boy. Mr. Saunders, get him a warm cup of tea."*

*"I think I need something more than tea."*

"Mr. Saunders poured me a double scotch.

*"We heard what happened, Mr. Hughes. It was savage of them to take you out. Mr. Saunders told us about your experience. Are you sure you're all right?"* The archeology professor's question was sympathetic.

*"Better now—but I'd like to leave and head back up to Cambridge. Now I can't until they say it's okay."*

*"Baskerville hound, eh?"*

"Doc, that little fellow with the digging group tried to cheer the conversation up with a laugh, but the larger man beside him just turned away and went back to his stout.

*"Well, if it was, then he'll have no more problems with me. Hell was in that dog's eyes."*

*"I'm now a might concerned, as we are out there both day and night at the dig. But it's three against one and we are rather well-armed for mischief with spades and other utensils. We'll give a good account of ourselves. Yes, I think we can give a proper defense."*

*"Then swing hard because this beast easily came up to my neck."*

*"Good God! Come on Bill, surely...?"* Cabell interjected.

"I knew they watched my hand shaking as I raised my glass to my lips.

*"I'm just telling you. All I know is that I'm finished going out at night, even if there's a clear, moonlit, starry*

96

*sky."*

"I found myself just staring deep into the glass of amber-colored scotch. In the periphery of my vision I watched them look at one another. I knew they thought I was bonkers.

*"Hope this doesn't get around too much—not good for business, what there is of it this time of year,"* said Mr. Saunders.

*"Oh, look on the bright side, Mr. Saunders, the old Holmes dog should help. The people love that stuff."* Again the smaller guy was trying to keep up the humorous side.

*"Well, I don't like that type of crowd. They're spoilers of the moors."*

*"Right you are, Mr. Saunders. Our dig would also become a tourist jaunt. We've been at it hard out there and I feel that we're really onto a great location."*

*"Have you by chance, Professor, heard any of that howling that the farmers have been complaining about?"* asked Mr. Cabell.

*"Not a whimper."*

"His cohorts also shook their heads.

*"Tell you what, Mr. Hughes. Rest a bit and I would like to show you about the archeological world of the moors tomorrow. I mean, if you feel up to it. The boys have to go in town for some groceries and other things. You'll find it quite interesting—and you too, Mr. Cabell."*

*"Oh, no thank you, sir. I'm moving on to Ivybridge in the morning. I'm still trying to do a bit of family history, you see."*

*"Very well. Maybe next time. What about it, Mr. Hughes?"*

*"Well, I..."*

*"I'll be here late in the morning so you can have a*

97

*nice night and restful morning. We'll just take a nice slow pace, and we'll lunch in Princetown. But if you're not up to it I'll understand."*

*"Can you call in the morning first?"*

*"Of course, of course."*

"They left in one of their Land Rovers and Mr. Saunders went into the kitchen. My new companion, Wilfred Cabell, seemed to be very concerned about my condition.

*"Be careful, Bill, you're not looking strong to me. You had better go get a nice nap."*

*"You're right. Damn, I wish you were staying around a little longer until they let me go back."*

*"Well, I only have so much funds for my folly so I have to make the most of it. But look, here's my home phone. Let's try to stay in touch. I'll let you know if I find out anything of substance. Besides, even if I don't, I've dearly enjoyed your company."*

*"Thank you. Let me see your pen there—here is my number at the college and at home."*

*"Marvelous. We'll dine together again this evening. Now get on up to your room and lie down, man."*

"I took him up on the suggestion, Doc, and I passed out as I hit the couch pillow. No nightmare or anything. It was just a thankful, deep sleep."

# Chapter 10

"I woke up with still a mild headache, Doc. I damn well recall that, but the thumping was gone. I went down to the small dining room where Cabell was reading the newspaper at the table.

*"Now you look better, Bill, a bit haggard but a thousand times better. Seems that roast with cream potatoes is the ticket tonight."*

*"Sounds good to me."*

*"Did everything come out all right with the police today?"*

*"I guess so. They said that they have to find out something because of Clayton's situation, but you know what happened."*

*"Did you really see that, Bill? I mean..."*

*"They can tell me till this whole damn moor freezes over that I just saw a regular dog. I know what I saw. It was huge and for me, a black-and-white-facts old cop, those eyes were red as a car's back lights. They went right through my soul. I know what I saw."*

*"Damn, I wish I had been there."*

*"Oh no you don't. What I'm afraid of is that all this is going to catch up with me and then the nightmares will start."*

"That night I slept, but it was an uncomfortable slumber. I was seeing those red things. I awoke early and unrested, but at least I was hungry. Breakfast was steaming porridge. While I was eating, the phone rang at the bar and Mrs. Saunders came to the table.

*"It's for you, sir."*

*"Hello?"*

*"It's me, Mr. Hughes, Inspector Martin. Has Sergeant Hopkins arrived by chance?"*

*"No, I don't think so, but I'll ask."*

*"Oh, no, it's okay. He really hasn't had time to get there yet I guess. Anyhow, I think we've pretty well summed up what took place."*

*"Oh, is Clayton awake?"*

*"No, no—but what we found is what happened to both of you at the same time."*

*"What do you mean?"*

*"Seems the young lads and their hens spiked the scotch. Ever heard of Lysergic acid diethylamide? Damn long tongue twister—or 'acid' for short?"*

*"Yes. It's also called LSD back home."*

*"Well, my boy, when you and Clayton gulped that booze, you also took in an enormous amount of that mind-altering stuff. Actually you both may have saved those kids' lives—it would certainly done some serious damage to them had they tried that infernal experiment."*

*"What?"*

*"I'm afraid so. The doctor thinks that's why Clayton went down. Poor Clayton evidently drank more than his share—that's why he's knocked out. Now don't get me wrong, but perhaps that's why the dog you saw was more than a dog."*

*"Oh geez."*

*"Yes, and that's why you can't seem to throw off the hangover that hit you with just a few swigs of scotch. If those*

100

kids had really gotten into that cocktail, I think it would have killed someone. At least Clayton's doctor said that, and he also thinks you're a very lucky fellow, considering your age and all that."

"But the head was so big and those fucking eyes!"

"All from the drug, Mr. Hughes. The doctor said that it was probably one of those wild moor ponies. That's why the head seemed so large."

"I just can't..."

"Oh, by the way, will you do me a favor please? Tell Sergeant Hopkins to give me a ring when he arrives."

"Can I leave here now?"

"Oh yes. We feel all is in place now. Have a good trip. And again, thank you for your assistance, Mr. Hughes."

"Sure."

"Goodbye—and call us if you should ever need our assistance."

"Yeah okay, thanks."

"The phone clicked, and when I looked up both Mr. and Mrs. Saunders were staring at me. I tried to smile and went back to the table.

"Everything all right, Mr. Hughes?" The innkeeper poured some fresh coffee.

"I was exasperated, Doc, and worn out.

"Fine, just fine. I can leave whenever I want."

"Oh no—we'll be missing your company, Mr. Hughes."

Cabell quickly interjected, "I think he needs a break from all this."

"If it hadn't been for the professor's invitation, I would have been packed and been out of that place, Doc. I went back up to my room for a little more rest.

"I was awakened by the crunch of gravel in the driveway, and then a vehicle engine turned off. Shortly a knock came from the door. It was the innkeeper announcing I had company and I immediately thought of the police again. When I looked down I saw the archeologist was talking with Mrs. Saunders.

*"I forgot to call first, Mr. Hughes, I'm sorry."*

*"I'll get my coat, Professor, and be right down."*

"Doc, I was still drained and just didn't want to go, but I had made the commitment and trudged down the stairs wearing a fake smile.

"As we were bumping over the back roads, my host went into his own story.

*"I was in geology at first but became bored, so I went back to school and received a degree in archeology, which was always my first love. Took a ridiculous bad hit in pay, but I'm a bachelor so it doesn't take much for me to exist."*

*"Yeah, I exist like that too—always broke. Where are we going?"*

*"Oh, just a few spots. I brought a basket for lunch, then I'll get you back before it turns too cold. Marvelous day today, however, toasty warm for the moors. But there'll be a fog tonight. This area we are in dates back to the Mesolithic period and into the Neolithic Age, oh about 8000 B.C. to around the 3000 period. Later we move into the Bronze Age when most of these stone structures were built. That rock formation just over there is about in the 2500 to the 600 B.C. age. That's my specialty. The only sad thing about the moor is that it's so acid—hardly anything survives of our early ancestors. Very little pottery or bones, and any metal objects would have corroded first, so all we're really left with are the flint work and hunting tools."*

"We came into an area with small rocks mounded in circles.

*"These are called burial cairns. We think the bones or ashes were placed in these. Over there you can see a few mounds, those are burial mounds also. Different periods of man buried their loved ones in various fashions through the centuries, you see."*

*"How did they make a living in this place?"*

*"Oh, it was forested, but they learned about grazing. If you cleared the wood, wild animals would come to graze the grass and the kill would be easier. So it made sense to capture them, build stone walls, then make the animals content to graze. Thus domestication and animal stock farming became the way to go. No more hunting parties. Make the animals happy with food and there you were—your own farm. So the trees went and in came the pasture lands. Of course not all the moor was forest, but a substantial part might have been. They also mined tin here all through the various centuries. Some say hidden tunnels meander all over the place and that the robbers and highwaymen used them to hide their ill-gotten gains deep in those caverns. Millions in stashed gold are also part of the folklore. Of course this hurts archeology, as indiscriminate digging to us is a sacrilege."*

"On and on he went, but it was really interesting, Doc, and damn soothing. Eventually we found our way back to his site. He pulled out the lunch and we ate on a small table under the sagging tent next to the dig. We were alone except for the sleeping dog.

*"Who are your assistants, Professor?"*

*"The quiet one you met is John Spensor. He's just a hired fellow to help move the heavy stuff, sift the screen, and help at keeping things running. Barney Stockdale, he's working at the college with me and is very meticulous, which*

*I greatly admire."*

*"He sure is small for this type of work."*

*"Yes, he is. I think he likes the solitude out here...I'm sure his height problem has always been his cross."*

*"I can see that, but what are you digging for here?"*

*"I think it might have been a smallish hill fort, but it seems to have burials in it also. Very unusual."*

"As we munched on the sandwiches and sipped on beer, he related his love for the moors and how he wished he could spend more time here instead of teaching.

*"What college did you say you were with?"*

*"King's College in Cambridge."*

*"Good gracious, I'm lecturing at Queens'! We're neighbors!"*

*"Quite so, quite so. But Cambridge is so large I doubt we shall ever meet."*

*"Yes, the whole place is big all right, but I love it. Now, I just want to get out of here and back to what I came here to do."*

*"Yes, I heard of your experience, old boy. I got the whole story from Mrs. Saunders about those kids with some drugs of some sort."*

*"The cops say I drank LSD with liquor and that's why Clayton and I went off the deep end. But you know, Professor, I know what I saw, and it scared the crap out of me, and all I want to do is get out of here."*

*"Why can't you leave?"*

*"They were wanting to question me, but it's all over and tomorrow I'm past history—headed north."*

*"Good for you, Mr. Hughes."*

"As we sat there I noticed him go into a quiet period.

*"Funny how the moor affects people and the various*

*areas within its boundaries. Notice anything about this place that's different from where we drove to?"*

*"No, not really."*

*"There is not one sound. Not a bird, not a sign of life. No sheep, no wild ponies, no rabbits, not even the ravens. It's like a dead zone, and it's been like this from the time that we arrived. Makes the other chaps uneasy."*

*"Creepy, huh Professor?"*

*"Yes. We can go maybe two miles and then there is life again. It's really weird."*

"Suddenly I felt what he felt. It was downright lonely. There was not a sound, just light wind gusts that made the moor turf whisper. It was strange, Doc.

"He drove me back and we had a few pints and exchanged numbers so whenever he got back we could get together. He was an okay guy. Later, after he left, I made a beeline upstairs to get my things packed. Then went back downstairs and told Mr. Saunders that I would be leaving in the morning so he could total my bill. It felt good, Doc. I wanted to see Cambridge again and forget Mr. Conan Doyle's moors.

"That evening as I was checking my luggage, I stopped for a moment and looked out on the moor through my window. A deep, white mist was settling in the valleys and its cold, tentacle-like fingers began to wind around the tors. The words of the old Baskerville manuscript that was read to Holmes in the story about the bleakness of the heath crept in my memory: *'...I counsel you by way of caution to forbear from crossing the moor in those dark hours when the powers of evil are exalted.'*

"Out there somewhere was Jenny, cold and soon to be forgotten. Doc, I wanted her to be somewhere. Maybe in London. Oh, you know, working at an easy job and having some peace—and being much happier. But I knew she was out there. I didn't want to think of her deep under the mud. I just didn't want to think that way."

"That's perfectly understandable, Bill."

"But as I stared out there, what seemed like a small light blinked through the mist. I looked harder but it never reappeared. To ease all the hell of the past few days, I joked to myself it was Selden the convict signaling to the butler at the Baskerville Manor. I wanted no more mystery or problems—and I again thought of Jenny. How does just one occurrence sear a brand in one's mind, Doc? Just those few days with her... God, I wanted her to leave with me, Doc. I was hurting for her."

"That's okay. It's not an uncommon thing, Bill, to immediately bond with another so quickly. You found some comfort with her, Bill, and wanted to help her too. It's a noble trait. Nowadays it's a rare thing to take time to listen to another's problems. We always seem too busy with ourselves. I think of it as an act of mercy and kindness, that you did this for her. You must try as you can to take comfort in that fact. But let's move on, or is that all?"

"Hell no. It was only just beginning."

# Chapter 11

"I went down to supper. Cabell was gone and I sat alone with a nice pork chop. Some other gentleman who had come in before me was reading the paper at another table while a few of the locals were in the pub. The door opened and the young Sergeant Hopkins, Inspector Martin's lackey, came in. This time the suit was gone and he had on a uniform. He came over to my table.

"*Hello, Mr. Hughes. Enjoying dinner, sir?*"

"*Yes.*"

"*Mind if I join you? I don't know the other chaps in the pub.*"

"*Of course not. Please have a seat.*"

"*Snug fit in this cloth, I can tell you—been about a year or more since I tried this on. My wife really got a kick out of it. The pants can't button.*"

"*In all my days on the force I rarely saw a uniform that ever fit, Sergeant. One part or another never seemed to conform.*"

"*That's true, Mr. Hughes, either too big or too small, eh? I guess the inspector called you about the laboratory find. I mean the stuff in the bottle.*"

"*Oh yes.*"

"*Did that help clear up the nightmare a bit?*"

"*No. It wasn't the LSD, Sergeant. I saw something. But no matter—I'm out of here tomorrow so I've erased it from my mind. At least I'm trying to convince myself that it* was the spiked LSD acid. You can tell that to the inspector."

"Yes, I guess that's the way to look at it. Clayton is still out of it, however, but the doctor said he may eventually come around. But it's still a wee bit too early to tell if any permanent damage has hit him."

"Mrs. Saunders came up to check on the table and Hopkins ordered bean and potato soup. He then went on about it not being fair that he should be stuck out in the moors but that the inspector promised him it would only be a week at the most.

"How is that inspector to work for?"

"Oh, he's stickler for details. Never a minute's rest with him. The other day I had—"

"Suddenly the door literally crashed open, Doc. Two men rushed in. It was the local farmers Ferguson and Morse Hudson.

"Saunders, call the ambulance quick! Johnson is either seriously hurt or dead!"

"Calm down, lads. What do you mean?" The innkeeper reached for the phone behind the bar.

"He's about three miles down the road. As we were driving over here we saw a blinking glow just off the road, so we turned off to check it out and it was Johnson's lorry. He's down the road, I mean just off the road."

"Call the damn police, will you?" The other farmer quickly cut into the conversation.

"The young sergeant screeched the chair back and quickly went into the pub. His uniform made the panicked situation calm down.

"What's the trouble, boys?"

"Thank God," said one of the farmers. "My neighbor Sidney Johnson is lying next to his lorry. I swear it looks like the truck ran over him or something. He's a mess. Call the ambulance, damn it Saunders!"

"The young sergeant did a great job of taking control of the situation, Doc.

*"Do as he says, will you? Now take me to where your friend is—I'll follow you."*

"Stanley Hopkins came back to my table.

*"Can you help me? I mean help me preserve the scene. You know what I mean."*

"Jesus, Doc, here I was again deep in it and only hours away from leaving the place. Damn if I wasn't riding in a police car once more as we followed the truck with the two farmers through the deep, steel gray fog. After about twenty minutes they turned off the road onto a field road that went about a hundred feet. Their headlights then picked up the red truck with its left turn signal blinking. Hopkins grabbed a flashlight from the backseat.

*"Get the other torch, Mr. Hughes, and don't let them tramp all over the place."*

"Hopkins went toward the truck and asked them to show him where the victim was lying. Slowly exiting their lorry, the two farmers approached the silent red vehicle, then abruptly stopped and pointed toward the front truck.

*"Okay, gentlemen, please don't go any closer until I can see what we have. Please."*

"Sergeant Hopkins' light beam disappeared into a glazed haze. One of the farmers finally broke the deep silence that rested over the moor as he turned to his companion. I was now standing with them and could see the cold vapor come from his mouth as his words formed.

*"I think Sidney is dead, Morse. Are you a policeman too, Yank?"*

*"Used to be."*

*"Oh, I see."*

*"What's taking him so long?"*

"The red lorry light going off and on made the whole area seem like a glowing fire, quickly rising and falling. Then we heard a gagging noise, and the young sergeant came back. Doc, he was as white as the collar on your shirt.

*"Mother of God! He wasn't run over."*

One of the farmers announced his thoughts, *"I thought maybe the truck somehow got him, you know, ran him over while he was checking the engine or something. Officer? Is he dead?"*

*"Yes. You two stay here. Come on over here, Mr. Hughes, if you will."*

"With the dead man's front truck lights out and only a turn signal flashing, our flashlights split in different directions with each wave of the moor mists. Then we both aimed the enormous beams on the prone man at the same time.

*"Jesus!"*

*"What in the hell happened to him, Mr. Hughes?"*

*"Damn it, call me Bill! I'm not that old, son—I'm sorry, it's just been awhile since I've seen things like this."*

*"I've never seen a man like this before in the eight years I've been on the force, Mr. Hughes—I mean Bill."*

"The country man lay about three feet from the right front wheel. The entire throat, part of the collar bone, and the lower jaw were just ripped and torn to shreds. His eyes were as wide open in death as I have ever seen. His arms and hands, Doc, were lying twisted and turned in an unnatural manner, but the thing that hit me about them was that they were also just mush.

*"Do you think what's left of his hands are defensive wounds, Bill?"*

*"God knows. I've seen some weird things in New York but never encountered anything like this before."*

"Sergeant Hopkins once more bent over the mauled man,

110

then his stomach again tried to retch as he spotted the light around the corpse.

"*Good God! Look there.*"

"Doc, I almost went bananas, but somehow kept my cool. As he swept the beam over the muddy ground there were a few footprints, but mostly the prints were of an animal.

"*I think they are animal prints, Mr. Hughes—I mean Bill. It looks like an animal foot pad...or like a wolf.*"

"*I'll say, and damn big steps too. And don't tell me they don't look like dog impressions to you?*"

"*I don't want to say so, but by God they do. It's his prints and the animal's. The ground is all smudged as if there was a terrific row going on here.*"

"*You need to call this in now before the scene becomes stale. Worse yet, if those two fellas leave and put out the word, the locals will be crawling all over the place. Go tell them it's vital that they keep their mouths shut so the investigation can begin. It won't do very much good, as I've experienced, but it'll give you time to get your boys in to look at the scene.*"

"*You're right.*"

"He went over and I could hear him talking to the men. I bent over and retched myself, Doc. The impact of whatever grabbed him was so vicious that when I stood back up my mind saw that damned hound trying to get in the car window. I began to shake, Doc, physically shake. The cold, the fog, the red glow on the victim's ripped flesh was making me shake. Then I heard the farmers' truck start and it kicked me out of the involuntary trance. Suddenly I heard the sergeant yell at them not to leave yet as the investigation team would need their statements. The two witnesses turned their truck back off and just stayed inside for the warmth. As I went back to the small patrol car, I heard Hopkins on his radio calling the dispatcher for backup and trying to give the location.

"My light again fell on the ground. Those animal footprints were easily six or more inches big, and again I found myself sweeping the area with the light.

*"Do you have a gun, Stanley?"*

"I couldn't hear his response.

*"Can't hear you, Stanley! I said do you have a gun with you?"*

*"Yes, in the trunk."*

*"Well, get it out and load it for God's sake!"*

"I heard the slamming of the trunk. He came back with a pistol, and once more we approached the bloody figure.

*"What's up? Did you hear something?"*

*"No, but I feel a damned bit safer with that near me."*

*"You really don't think that...?"*

*"I don't want to think it, but I want you next to me with that gun."*

"It was so bitter cold, Doc, that we went back to the car and warmed ourselves. As I think back now, it seemed like forever before three cars and a van pulled up behind us.

"I looked out my window and who did I see, but that same Inspector Martin.

*"Bloody hell, not you again?"*

"I rolled down my window and gave him a juicy smile.

*"Yes. I happened to be in the neighborhood, Inspector."*

"As he walked away I heard him mumble, *"Smart ass yank."*

*"Oh Inspector,"* I yelled, *"you may want to take some pictures of the impressions around the man—looks like large Chihuahua prints to me."*

"I was taken back to the inn and once more told by the

112

policeman to stay put until the inspector came in for a talk. Son of a bitch, I could not leave that place even if I wanted to! It just would not let me go. By this time I was thinking, *To hell with Cambridge and the whole island! I just want to go back home.* I had left the world of violence when I signed the retirement papers. I was happier than I have ever been in the intervening years—now I was thrown back into this pit. Into the hellish pit of Dartmoor."

# Chapter 12

"When I walked into the pub, both Mr. and Mrs. Saunders were at the bar and the barrage of questions came full force.

*"Was it Mr. Johnson then, Mr. Hughes?"*

*"I think so."*

*"And how did the accident happen?"*

*"I wish I knew. Sergeant Hopkins wouldn't let me get near the scene when I arrived."*

"My lie let me off the hook with the questions and I went back up to my room. After two scotches I thought I'd go back down and try to get something else to eat as I never did finish my dinner. But then I wondered—after seeing what I had seen—whether I could hold my meal down. As I went to the top of the steps, I saw that the pub was beginning to fill with the locals—the news had already gotten out like a wildfire. Realizing I was the only one there who had been at the scene, I knew I would be interrogated to the fourth degree. With no hope for a peaceful meal, I went back to my room and opened the bottle for dinner.

"I guess it was about two hours later when a small tapping at my door woke me from my liquid-induced sleep.

*"Come in."*

"It was the young sergeant, Hopkins.

*"Hello, sir. Mind if I come in? Oh, I'm sorry, I think I woke you up, sir?"*

*"It's okay, Sergeant, please come in. Need some refreshment? Oops, it's empty!"*

*"Oh no, thank you anyway, sir. On the job you know, and you know who is downstairs giving the news to the pub gang as best he can. Doesn't want to let too much out you see, but he said he owed it to the locals to keep them advised. He asked me if you could come with me out the back door to the car so he can have a chat with you."*

*"A chat?"*

*"Yes. Underneath all his bravado I think the inspector respects you as a New York criminal investigator."*

*"He checked on me, huh?"*

*"Yes, sir. Found you were in the bureau just like our CID. Homicide were you, Mr. Hughes?"*

*"Yes, and way too long. I wanted a nice promotion out of there, but it never came so I took my years and left. Besides homicide is nothing but drug-related now. Nasty stuff, and worse, the scum are mindless animals."*

*"Yeah...I can see that. Well, shall we go, sir?"*

*"Okay, let me grab my coat."*

"We literally tiptoed down the back steps and went to the inspector's car, which was parked behind the inn. Another officer was at the wheel—the inspector's new bobby chauffeur.

*"I'll go back inside now, Mr. Hughes, I mean Bill. He'll be along shortly."*

"And it was shortly, because just as Hopkins went in Inspector Martin came out. Some of the locals came out too but headed to their vehicles.

*"Thank God that's over. Start the car, Peters. I need the heat."*

*"Yes, sir."*

*"Well, well—it seems wherever I turn there you are, Mr. Hughes."*

*"Yes, but if I can go back to Cambridge, I'll be gone*

*tonight.*"

*"Indeed, I rather bet you would. But to be honest—Oh Peters, go in the pub and warm up if you will."*

"The officer obeyed and we were alone in the backseat. God, the cop cars are small in England.

*"You got there first, Mr. Hughes, with Hopkins?"*

*"Yes."*

*"Sergeant Hopkins is new meat to CID. He's basically a newcomer, so I was wondering if you noticed anything when you arrived that he might have missed by any chance?"*

*"Only that those footprints and the ground were really damp. The footprints make some sort of weird sense, but the wetness—that's what's eerie as far as I'm concerned. It was high ground."*

*"Yes, I saw that too, Mr. Hughes."*

*"And it hadn't rained, just a deep fog, so to speak."*

*"Anything else?"*

*"Yeah. Whatever got him pulled his neck, upper torso, and jaw out. It's no accident with brake slippage or whatever. He wasn't run over because everything would have been pressed down."*

*"That's what I wanted to hear. Hopkins didn't pick up on that, but somehow I knew you would."* He paused. *"I want you to know I'm probably going to have to suggest a pack of dogs got him, but then again, I am uneasy with that."*

*"Then why have me here?"*

*"Because tomorrow the press will descend on this village and they are going to go for you. Especially with you being a Sherlock Holmes enthusiast and policeman too. The Baskerville hound will no doubt make a debut. The press will eat it up."*

*"So what do you want me to do?"*

*"I would be obliged if you would stay clear, Mr. Hughes. Then they'll get their sensational morsels and head back. If you were here they would really get excited, and I need them out of here so I can proceed."*

*"Okay, let me leave tonight. I'm out of here."*

*"No, no, can't do that. You are one of the first observers so the inquest will want to make reservations for you."*

*"Oh come on, Inspector—can't I come back for that?"*

*"Rather you not, ole boy. Just stick around."*

*"Am I under suspicion by any chance, Inspector?"*

*"Heavens no, just stay awhile on my expense at the inn."*

"He immediately changed the subject and lit a cigarette.

*"Wish I could quit these damn things. The American Indian's gift to the world, eh? But getting back to the subject at hand...It's that dammed wet ground that has me puzzled a bit."*

*"Yes. But what about the animal prints?"*

*"I'm having impressions made—damn big prints for sure."*

*"Maybe I wasn't hallucinating that night after all?"*

*"Well, if a dog and his pack are around, they'll be hunted down. I'm having a chopper come over the moor tonight with a heat sensor. That'll locate the pack. Seems these dogs like to hunt at night. The chaps in the pub told me in no uncertain words that the slaughter of the animals about the moors has been more frequent than usual lately."*

*"Yes, so I've heard."*

*"I'm running forensic tests on the corpse too. Maybe*

*something is in all that body mess."*

*"Good idea. But you keep saying 'dogs.' I saw only one that night with Clayton. And what about the red eyes?"*

*"Oh, now I believe you saw something, but the LSD makes the mind see Technicolor. In any case, if it's a pack of dogs, we'll get them tonight or tomorrow when the game wardens come in. Now the whole area will be on my arse to clear this up quick. Besides, with the reverend's wife missing, and this dead farmer, all hell is headed my way. Mind you, I believe in reality and no mystical Baskerville hound crap—and I hope to God you are with me on that matter. We don't need the black arts on this case. Lord, they're gonna be on my butt. Ever had your chaps come down on you really hard, Mr. Hughes?"*

"The inspector rolled down the window and flicked his cigarette out.

*"Almost got canned by my superiors on three cases, so yes, I've been there many times on the New York streets."*

*"Yes, I'm sure. Well, goodnight Bill—can I call you Bill?—and do hide away for me tomorrow like a good lad, won't you?"*

*"My pleasure. But I want out of here."*

*"Yes, yes. I promise you'll be on your way in a day or two at the most."*

"Doc, as I stood outside and watched the police car fade into the black, I looked over toward the indenture just off the road. That trail was always Jenny's path. I crossed over the deserted road and walked down the footpath. The fog clouding the ground was ghostly, but I didn't feel afraid for some reason. I distinctly have that in my mind, Doc. I was half expecting Jenny to appear out of the mist, but all I heard was unfamiliar chirping calls deep with in the moor and bogs.

"I awoke the next morning, and when I opened the blinds a more beautiful day in England could not be imagined. It was almost like a spring day instead of the colder month. I was ready to get out of the place, so I decided to bicycle all day in order to hide from the reporters as requested by Inspector Martin. As I dressed, I spotted a note on the floor that had been pushed under the door. The envelope read 'Mr. Hughes.' The message was written in longhand.

*Dear Sir,*
*I am Morse Hudson, the owner of the farm not far from where Mr. Sidney Johnson's is located. About a mile away on the same road. Me and the missus would be honored if you would take time and stop for tea today. Look for the yellow cottage. I'll be around the place if you can get over. I think we may have something in common.*
*Thank you for your time,*
*Morse*

"I wondered, *Something in common?*

"Well, Doc, if I was going to ride, that was just as good as any place to head toward. The press would be gathering shortly, so I hurried down to grab some breakfast. Mrs. Saunders served the steaming hot oatmeal and coffee.

*"Terrible business last night, Mr. Hughes. All these goings on are giving me the frights, I can tell you that for sure."*

*"Yes, but I'm sure they'll have it straightened out in no time."*

*"All night that helicopter going over. I thought we were finished with that when the young lady disappeared. And now early this morning the men are out with hunting dogs. It's just awful. I hope they get the wild beasts*

119

*that did those horrors."*

*"I'm sure they will, Mrs. Saunders."*

"By nine o'clock I was finished. Then came the sound of dogs barking as trucks and cars pulling up in the drive gave me the signal to head out. As I rode off, a television news van drove into the drive, with three cars behind it. The press was descending like a feeding frenzy upon the small hamlet. More cars passed me on the road and turned into the small hotel.

"As I coasted down the small road, the morning air was fresh and brisk but not bone-chilling cold. It was a good day. My mind wandered over the tors rising in the background. The granite rocks rising like jagged castles or crooked teeth crowned the earth mounds. The gentle roll of the hills displayed ruddy, low-growing vegetation in shades of gray, brown, violet, and copper. A rabbit skirted across the road while the inevitable ravens circled overhead. It was peaceful until a helicopter zoomed overhead. The hunt was on for the wild moor dogs. I then wondered about Jenny as I looked at the rocky hill. *Where are you?* Still I peddled without effort until I had to puff my way up a small rise in the road; then I spotted the yellow cottage. It was neat as farms go. There was a certain pride about the home and front garden grounds, but the barn and other out sheds were typical. Half of the out buildings were in good shape; the others nearly falling down from disrepair.

"Before I could even knock on the door, it opened. A heavyset, serious-looking woman greeted me as best she could.

*"You be Mr. Hughes?"*

*"Yes, ma'am."*

*"Morse said you may be stopping by—he's over in the barn. I have to leave so you'll have to have tea with him. It's a sad, sad day. I'm off to help pack up Mrs. Johnson. She wants out of here, God help her. She wants to sell and go be with her daughter in Plymouth."*

*"Yes, it was terrible about Mr. Johnson. A tragedy for your whole community."*

*"Well, I can tell you I'm not far behind the poor lady. Too many unnatural things going on—I think God has never been fond of this moor. My husband is stubborn, but I can tell he's about to give in he is, and now with this happening to Sidney last night and the other scary stuff, well, I can see it in his eyes. He's just not as sure as he used to be. Anyway, you make yourself at home, Mr. Hughes. Like I said, he's over in the barn, but if you have mind to wait inside I can give a tug on the bell and he'll come over."*

*"Oh no, please. I'll make my way over there, and thank you very much. Aren't any biting dogs around are there by chance?"*

*"Oh no, last one we had disappeared."*

"Doc, I liked the farm, the smell, the chickens clucking around, and the sudden squeal of some pigs not getting along. It was a nice, clean country feeling, and when I opened the small inset door to the barn I saw a figure in the back with a cow. There was just one cow in the sable. A few chickens fluttered by me as I stuck my head in the doorway.

*"Mr. Hudson?"*

*"That be you, Mr. Hughes? Do come in, sir."*

"He was one of the men who were regularly at the pub—his pipe was sending blue waves through the sparkling hay-scented air.

*"I appreciate you taking time to come out, Mr. Hughes. No doubt the inn is a beehive by now."*

*"Yes, it was just beginning when I left."*

*"Care to go to the house, or can you just take a seat here on a stool?"*

*"Oh, a stool is fine."*

"He was smearing a clear goo of what looked like Vaseline

on the cow's neck.

*"Rose here was near killed a few weeks ago, Mr. Hughes. See, she's all stitched up."*

"A long black line bordered by pink skin was easily obvious. The hair had been shaved and dark thread was interlaced against a dark purple streak. A sliver of crimson flesh accented the cruel-looking cut.

*"You mentioned about something we had in common, Mr. Hudson?"*

*"Yes. I was reluctant to bring this up after what happened to you and Constable Clayton. But it's no secret any more about what happened to you, Mr. Hughes, so don't be shocked. It's a small community hereabouts and the young Officer Hopkins is talkative when he has a pint or two."*

*"I see. So you know about what happened to us?"*

*"Aye sir, I do. But now as to what happened to Sidney last night, well, I knew I had better get things said because I have a bad feeling about what's going on around here. Oh, I was going to talk to the regular officers but then I knew what they would say after I told them what happened. They would say I stayed too long at the pub and then went home pie-eyed. But when I heard about your experience from the chaps at the bar...and then you being an old copper—I mean policeman—from America...well, I just thought maybe we could compare to see if we weren't both going daft."*

*"To be honest, Mr. Hudson, they have me wondering if I saw anything but a puppy crossing the road."*

*"Yeah, so I heard. Hopkins spilled that too about you and Clayton getting into the bottle and it was spiked with some drug or whatever. Now be true, Mr. Hughes, do you in your God-given mind really think that what you saw*

was real, or was it that concoction you drank with Clayton?"

"No. I saw what I saw."

"Well, that's about as straight as an answer as can be given. So you say what you saw was not a phantom of the mind?

"Yes. But what is this about?"

"I'll tell ya, sir, but first, would you trust me? If you could let me in on what happened to you, then as God's witness I'll reveal what happened to me."

"Why not? I thought, Doc. What's to lose or gain? So I went through the whole episode again as he sat on a hay bale all the while puffing on the old pipe. As I ended the story, the cow mooed as if to bring down the curtain on my confusing words.

"I believe every word as if it were gospel, Mr. Hughes. I know you think of me as just a country local who has a pint or two and has been raised on a diet of Dartmoor myths, but I am a God-fearing Christian, Mr. Hughes. I don't believe in fairy stories, let alone Baskerville and Dartmoor hound legends. But now..." Morse hesitated. "...But now, I'm sorta shaken. Mind you, I have prayed over the thing that happened to me, but now as it has happened to you, well, maybe by some chance there is more than what meets the eye so to speak."

"Yes—I believe in black and white too, but damn it, a dog did appear to me. I know it wasn't drugs, and poor Clayton is out of it. I just know it wasn't the drugs! I—"

"Easy, Mr. Hughes, no need to get excited—though I've been shaken myself, and now the missus wants me to see a doctor. But I can honestly tell you that it wasn't any drink on my part either."

"Doc, when he made that statement, I felt like I was hit with a baseball bat."

# Chapter 13

""*What do you mean, Mr. Hudson?*"

"*About three weeks ago I was awakened by the howls that had been plaguing us here for months on end. They'd also been heard around the Johnsons' and Fergusons' farms from time to time and were driving us all crazy. The wives were scared I can tell you—they started in with the legends and all the rubbish that went with the tale. Heaven knows we tried to get Clayton to stop the dog cries, but he never could. Now when I heard what happened to you and Clayton with those kids, I thought well maybe it would come to an end. But it hasn't and we still hear the damn howls every now and then. It's such an eerie sound, Mr. Hughes—it sort of drifts about the dark so to speak.*

"*But to get back to what happened those few weeks ago, it must have been about two o'clock in the morning when I heard the wailing. My wife was terrified I can tell you. I was fed up, so I grabbed my shotgun, put my boots on with a coat over my night clothes, and went out. Me wife was all upset for sure, but I was determined. The barn door was open and when I snapped the light on, my Rose here wasn't there. I was worried for the ole girl and headed toward the sound. It seemed to be coming from near the tor that rises not far from me farm. I didn't want to turn me torch on until I was near the noise, then I could give the dog a good blast. I had been walking up the rise for about a good half-*

hour...then I heard it again. It was just one dog, but God help me, what a horrible wail!

"Mind you, I was shaken something terrible, but what made my blood chill, Mr. Hughes, was suddenly I heard old Rose bellowing—she was there also and her call was desperate. A farmer can tell an animal call, Mr. Hughes, and Rose was crying for help. I stumbled, sir, and with the rocks falling against one another, it gave my secrecy away because the dog howling stopped. But poor Rose here was going crazy. I was at a race and pointed the light to see her lying on the ground just under a stone chunk. She was flaying her legs and crying out so loud that I was trembling for her. As I got to her I could see that just near her neck was a huge tear and she was bleeding so bad. The meat had been torn out and my old girl couldn't stop trying to raise her head. Christ's saints, her eyes had such fear and a pleading about them. I laid me gun down and took off my jacket, then my night shirt to place over the wound to stop the bleeding. All the while I was talking to her and trying to calm her down. She knew I was there, Mr. Hughes—it sounds crazy, but she knew I was there for her. She finally settled down and stopped her mooing, but her breathing was beyond description. She was heaving, Mr. Hughes. I knew I had to get her up quick and down to the farm and get help. The vet is over in Ashburton, and if we could only make it to the barn she might could live. I'll be honest, sir, I started getting emotional so to speak. There are certain animals that one loves you see, and Rose was special if you know what I mean."

"Of course, Mr. Hudson. We're all animals aren't we?"

"That's it sir—we're all flesh and blood together.

*Well, as I got her up, she of course stumbled around a bit, but she stood there as if composing herself, but still trembling. It began misting, Mr. Hughes, you know just a light wet fog, and it was causing me torch to glisten against the moist rocks. I was reaching for me light that was on the ground when I saw it, Mr. Hughes. I saw it as sure as you are sitting across from me."*

"Yes?"

*"I mean I didn't see the thing itself—I saw a red glow reflected on the rock. It was like two red dots, and when I turned to see where they came from, it wasn't there. I was scared to hell and back, I can tell you true. But as I was coaxing Rose to take a step, then a most God-awful growl, if I can call it that, came from somewhere. It was so deep and terrifying, Mr. Hughes, that I almost left everything—and I mean Rose too—and started to run. It wasn't the same sound what I heard coming up to the tor; it was like a beast within hell roaring. Rose's eyes were as wide as mine, I can tell you that. Then, even over Rose's heavy panting, I heard an even deeper breathing. Another horrible grumble came with almost a hissing sound. I was so terrified, Mr. Hughes, my heart was in my throat. Again I caught a glancing red streak across the wet boulder and I turned, but whatever it was, was gone again. All the while I was pulling on poor Rose's rope, pleading with her to move, when she could only take a few steps at a time.*

"Then some small rocks trickled down from atop the biggest granite spire. And when I looked up, I saw it, Mr. Hughes. It was staring down at me. It was blacker than the night and those eyes...those eyes...!"

"Now it's your turn to calm down, Mr. Hudson."

"Doc, the old man had tears rolling down from within his

glasses. Then he raised them, gently wiped them off with a rag from his back pocket, and began again. He was quiet for a while, then tapped his pipe as if to take a break from his episode. I let him gather himself and we were both silent for a few minutes. Finally he was ready to continue.

*"I was dumbstruck, Mr. Hughes. All I could do was just stare back. I didn't want to, but it had me—it had me like in a trance. I was wanting to scream, but it was looking at me so penetratingly with those eyes that I could not move or make a sound. Then, as if a mirage, Mr. Hughes, the gigantic thing turned around and left the top of the rock. I had to sit down and collect myself. Poor Rose was weaving back and forth, and I was whining like a child—even my nose was running. I have never felt fear like that in my life— and I have been in heavy combat, mind you—but this was a throbbing fear that went to the roots of me very soul."*

*"I felt it too, Mr. Hudson. I understand."*

*"Yes, I see you do."* He paused a moment to calm down a little. *"Please, call me Morse. Whether we like it or not, this thing has brought us together."*

*"Certainly, Morse, and call me Bill. But go on please."*

*"I was a mess. I picked up the shotgun, but I can say I was trembling so bad that it was useless in my hands. I think I even dropped it and picked it up again. Rose was bellowing again, and suddenly, as if the very gates of hell slammed shut, all was quiet. Not a sound. It was like Rose and me were the only two beings in the world. I waited and waited for something. What I was waiting for, I'm not sure. Then from way in the distance that same demon howl came reverberating through the hills. Rose and I were so alone, it was as if no other creature existed in the world. It took us*

*almost until light to get back. My wife had called Sidney Johnson and he was just driving up when I came into the back gate. I went on that some dogs got to Rose, and Sidney helped me medicate her the best we could and we put her in the barn. Sidney then left.*

*"My wife knew I was lying. She said I was so pale that I almost glowed and that I couldn't stop quivering. She called the vet, Bill, and my missus put me to bed. The next day I got so drunk that I couldn't get out of the house—she knew something more than just a pack of dogs happened, but I kept to the story until now. I'm sorry I got so emotional, but it has set itself like a branding iron on my soul, Bill. I seldom get emotional like this, at least not since the war."*

*"You don't have to apologize to me, Morse. If anyone is with you and Rose, it's me. As far as I know, only the three of us are alive to tell about it. I can't count Clayton. I'm not sure if he'll come through it all."*

*"Then it was not a hallucination, Bill? You saw and felt the same thing?"*

*"Good God, yes! Only worse—I passed out from the fright. You stayed on your feet. Can we have that tea now? I feel like you're completely exhausted—I know I was after it happened to me."*

"Doc, we didn't say another thing all the way to the cottage. We knew we were alone with such an experience. He wanted to sell the farm and move on, and I wanted to go home.

"But you know what, Doc? Suddenly, as I was riding home, a thought just came crashing into my pea brain. If both of us saw it, then it was no mirage, no phantom—it was real. Someone, somehow, found the largest dog in the whole world and—like the villain Stapleton in Conan Doyle's Baskerville story—had brought the beast to Dartmoor. Then again, it was simply impossible—no dog could ever be that enormous. It had to be a case of theatrics. Whoever had masterminded that fiendish monster was after something, just like Stapleton was after the Baskerville estate. Still, I could not believe God made a dog with a head as big as a lion's head, but the thought was now in place. Somebody had to be the cause of this whole mess. It simply could not just be a mind-blowing legend coming to life. Reality is reality, it just had to be. Then again…those scarlet eyes and that hideous sound… Doc, my mind was whirling trying to find an answer. What really topped it off was the dates of when these events happened. It was the same month that Sherlock Holmes became involved with the Baskerville case. Between the dog and the dates, my old cop instinct really started to boil.

"When I arrived at the inn it was packed. Reporters and the locals were going at it, but I managed to squeeze myself to the bar for a pint. Over in the corner was the archeologist group around a table. The professor gave me a wave, stood up, and came over next to me.

*"We may be pulling out until all this blows over, Mr. Hughes. Besides the boys are on edge now. We also heard a baying for the first time the other night. Maybe we all need a break."*

*"I certainly understand. I'm desperately trying to get out too, but the damn inspector has me staying until the inquest. I have to answer questions about when we found Mr. Johnson."*

*"Oh yes. Were there really dog prints around him as I've been hearing around the pub here?"*

*"You bet, and damned big ones too."*

*"Well, I wish you luck, Mr. Hughes."*

"I watched him head back to the table with a refilled glass. Over against the other wall was one of the farmers I had seen with Morse Hudson and the now-slaughtered Sidney Johnson. It was

Ferguson, and he was shaking his finger in the face of another local as if making a strong point. Then the pub door opened and, of all people, the rock kid and his consorts came in followed by his father and mother. The reporters immediately swarmed the kid while the father came over my way.

"Still here are you, Mister?"

"Oh yes, still around."

"We couldn't miss this publicity, it was just too good. Terrible event, we're upset about the tragedy. But business is business, and with the recent film of my son on the moors, the black thing in the video flick...well, we thought we might return for some press."

"It seems to have worked well."

"You'll excuse me. I got to get over there to make sure what he says won't hurt the dead bloke's family's feelings. It's a sure tragedy."

"Doc, if ever an insincere statement was made by anyone I have ever interrogated in my years, that guy was the epitome of 'I don't give a shit. It's the bucks that count and everybody has got to move out of the way.'

"After a few minutes the ruckus was getting to me. As I was trying to head upstairs, I saw Mrs. Saunders stick her head out of the kitchen door.

"Oh, Mr. Hughes, there's a call for you. You had better take it back here in the kitchen. It's way too noisy at the bar."

"Thank you, ma'am."

"The kitchen aroma was delicious as I put the phone to my ear.

"That you, Mr. Hughes?"

"Yes."

"Inspector Martin here. Can you hear me? It's a

131

*bad connection."*

*"Yes, Inspector?"*

*"The inquest will be held in Exeter on Monday. I'll send someone to pick you up. Then you can trot north, Mr. Hughes."*

*"Thank you, Inspector."*

*"Oh, by the bye, thought I'd pass this on to you. Seems forensics found dog saliva on the victim's cuffs, plus around his shirt collar and where there were other bite indentations. You know the defensive wound stuff? He was evidently trying to protect himself and not caught by surprise from the back or anything like that. The attack was found to be a straight-on frontal assault."*

*"So it was a dog attack."*

*"Well, it seems so. There were dog hairs on his clothes, but they were not identifiable to any known pedigree. But the doctor who examined him said the teeth were unusually sharp."*

*"Yes. Do you recall when I said that I saw the dog with Clayton that its teeth were so sharp that they glistened? And also that it had like an iridescent foam about its mouth?"*

*"Just so, but I can't go into that, Mr. Hughes. Remember there were extenuating circumstances in your case. The bottle and the LSD and all."*

*"I'm just telling you what I saw, that's all."*

"I was again put down by the inspector, Doc.

*"Yes, yes—well, to be truthful, it's all over. The helicopter boys shot three large dogs along the Abbot's Way path. They got them today. We'll be bringing them by the inn for the locals and the press to see in the morning. Big old things."*

132

*"But isn't Abbot's Way miles from here? It's too far south for them to have gotten there and not be seen by those search guys. It couldn't have been those mutts."*

*"Oh, I feel confident it was them all right. They got the culprits for sure."*

*"Would it be okay if I go over to Plymouth for the weekend, then be back for the inquest?"*

*"Oh certainly. Please enjoy yourself. See you in a few days, Mr. Hughes."*

"Doc, in my gut I knew that he knew it couldn't have been that pack of dogs. The inspector was like me on a case—you just hoped to hell you had the thing solved and it would go away. You weren't sure that all the facts were reasonable, but you just prayed that it would satisfy the district attorney's office.

*"Mind if I make a telephone call, Mrs. Saunders? It's to Cambridge. You can put it on my bill."*

*"Oh of course, Mr. Hughes. Help yourself."*

"She was busy with the oven and never even turned around. I called the college and got hold of the offices. They said that I could come back the next week as some of the classes were beginning to reopen. It was a relief, Doc. I was so ecstatic. I wanted to get the lectures over with and just take a vacation back here in good old New York. To be honest, I had had enough of Sherlock Holmes and the Baskerville hound, not to mention the moor."

# Chapter 14

"Take a break, Bill. Stand up and go in the refrigerator there. Get something to drink, stretch awhile."

----------- ----------- -----------

"Yeah, that's better, Doc. I needed to move. Well, to get back to where I left off, the brief holiday at Plymouth was wonderful. I knew I was still shaky and underneath just messed up, but I found an inexpensive hotel and meandered around the older part of town and antique shops. You know, nothing special, but the sea air was the nicest part. It was nippy, but the idea of so much sea history associated with the place helped me ignore the wind's bite. After a refreshing two days, I returned to The Red Bull late in the evening and retired to my room.

"On Monday morning I settled my hotel expenses with Mr. and Mrs. Saunders and packed my bags as I awaited the ride to the inquest in Exeter. The noonday moor has an earthy aroma about it, and it greeted me as the hotel door opened.

*"All ready to go this fine morning I see, Mr. Hughes?"* Sergeant Hopkins was to be my chauffeur.

*"Mind if I put my bags in the car, Sergeant? I'm catching the train out of Exeter."*

*"Back to Cambridge, eh?"*

*"Yes, thank God."*

*"You see all those folks around that lorry there, Mr. Hughes? They're showing off the three dogs that they shot along Abbot's Way."*

*"Mind if I take a look before we go?"*

*"No. Help yourself."*

"Doc, when I looked at those poor mangy dogs lying in the back of that truck, I almost died. The poor things were half starved and could not have even brought down a baby sheep, much less a human. I walked back to the constable's car and slammed the door.

*"What do you think, Mr. Hughes?"*

*"What do you think, Sergeant?"*

*"I think the Chief Inspector is desperate. When those farmers see those poor things they'll be some hell-raising going on for sure. Those boys will know it couldn't have been them. The Chief Inspector is trying to get the press off of him for a while."*

*"Yeah, I can understand that point. They're as vicious as the dogs."*

*"Well, we'll be in Exeter shortly and then it's over for you."*

*"Yes. That's a comforting thought. Then a few more weeks at Cambridge and I'm on that big bird home. I think I'll focus on* Alice in Wonderland *instead of Mr. Sherlock Holmes and the Baskerville Hound. God knows I've had my fill."*

"As we drove out of the driveway I looked over at the path that I last saw Jenny take before she disappeared. Somehow I was taking her with me. You know what I mean? Doc, can one person really get to you that quickly in life? This wasn't any love story novel. I knew I could have saved her, and I knew I could have made her happy if only there had been time. I fell so in love with her face and her voice. She'll always be with me, Doc. I mean—"

"Yes, yes—no need to go on. We've gone over this, Bill. Of course a single event can change a person. So why not Jenny for you? It was a tragedy, but as I said before, think of it in a positive way if possible. You at least met her, and you were probably the nicest thing that happened to her during her desperation. She, in a unique way, belongs to you now, Bill. Keep her. But try to think you were blessed just to have known her for even so short a time, and mostly that you showed her a kind of tenderness. Maybe that will help."

"That doesn't work, Doc. You sound like a priest. I want her now—with me. I think my unrest has as much to do with her as with any of the events. I want her back, Doc. I want her back in the worst way."

"I quite understand, but let's try to get back, Bill. What happened after you arrived in Exeter?"

"I was sworn in and made my statement before the magistrate. Their inquest is not like ours; it's sort of like a jury system. The jury decides whether a crime was committed. Inspector Martin was there of course. And Sergeant Hopkins just echoed what I said to the jury. I didn't wait around for the ruling, which I'm sure was going to be an attack by a pack of wild dogs. I caught a cab and headed to the train station. I was out of there, Doc. I left the hell behind—at least that's what I thought as the train lurched forward.

"After switching in London, I found myself in Cambridge late that evening. My room was comfortable again. The heat worked wonderfully and everything else. The school was back up and running. For the next few weeks I was in a marvelous, old, wood-cracked classroom.

"One unusual warm weekend, as I sat on a bench near the small, shallow River Cam, which runs through the town, I stopped reading for a moment and watched the small boats being slowly poled along by mostly students. They call it 'punting' over there. I was almost in the throws of a nodding nap when from some window came music—it was a person practicing on the piano, Doc. The melody would stop and start, and finally it continued. It was

Beethoven's "Moonlight Sonata." It was Jenny's song. Everything about her came back. Her unbelievably stunning face, her hair whirling in the moor breeze, her sitting at the piano, and me being allowed to see her tears. It hurt so deep. The pain of her no longer being in my life just buried itself deeper and deeper with every refrain that came from the unknown window. I was glued to the lawn-seat. Then the music stopped. I wanted more, but it disappeared just as my Jenny had done. As God is my witness, of all that I have told you, Doc, I remember that moment more than anything.

"Except for a few wrenching nightmares about that dog and seeing Jenny on the moor, I was managing my emotions. At least I thought I was. I had only about three more weeks and I was going home. I traveled to Ely to see the cathedral, and even ventured way out of the way over a weekend to see the Brontë Parsonage. You know, it's where the three sisters lived who wrote those classic novels—*Wuthering Heights*, *Jane Eyre*, and others. The only bad part of that trip was that their town sat on another moor. I didn't even leave the small village. I hated the moor countryside."

"Hmmm, I can understand that. Go on."

"Then it was just as if the never-ending bad dream happened all over again, Doc. I mean what occurred next was so unbelievable that I thought I was in another dimension or something. Devon and Dartmoor came back to attack and haunt me. It was on a Sunday morning. I had strolled down to a small cafe and glanced at the newspaper on a side table as I paid for a roll and coffee.

"Doc, I must have changed colors at the counter because the hostess asked me if I was feeling all right. I lifted up the paper and the headlines read something like "Second farmer killed by wild dogs at Dartmoor." I sat down and read it as if I was starving. The words rushed into my brain. It was Ferguson—Robert Ferguson, the farmer, whom I had last seen at the pub. Ferguson who was friends with Sidney Johnson and Morse Hudson. I was almost in a state of shock."

"I can see why—it's uncanny all right. Go ahead, Bill."

"It went on to say that the postman had a special package delivery or something like that, and when he couldn't get an answer at the door, he went around the back of the farmhouse to see if Ferguson was in his barn. As he turned the corner of the house he saw Ferguson with his sheepdog next to him. Both of them were mangled and their throats were savagely attacked. The grounds were covered in faint dog prints. If I remember correctly, the call was for more reinforcements and air searches, and an all-out intensive hunt for the vicious creatures was taking place. It said something about three dogs of a menacing canine pack had already been destroyed. Doc, I recall laying down the paper and almost laughing. I think I shocked the girl because I unconsciously said a loud, 'Dogs? My ass!'

"I went outside to take gulp of fresh air and to calm myself and then went back inside. I consumed the article for every detail and then slowly put the newspaper down. My coffee cup was vibrating as I put it to my lips.

*"Mind if I have a look at it?"* An older gentleman was at the next table.

*"Of course not. Please help yourself."*

*"You look like you've seen a ghost, my boy?"*

*"I've just read about the recent tragedy on Dartmoor."*

*"Oh yes, I see it's here. I used to dig at Dartmoor many years ago. Too old now—the dampness gets to me. Now I just teach book archeology at King's College. I rather think I put many a fine student to napping during my lectures, but I hope I'm passing on a bit of something to them anyway."*

*"What a coincidence! I met one of your fellow*

*excavators at Dartmoor—he and his crew were digging while I was visiting there recently. His name was...it was—damn, I think I've forgotten it. Oh yes, it was Latimer. Harold Latimer."*

*"Who?"*

*"Harold Latimer. He has some kind of grant or something. Been there awhile too. He really seemed to know his stuff."*

*"I've been at King's for over 30 years. Never heard of a Latimer."*

*"Harold Latimer. He's with two other men. One is, let's see...what was his name? He's at your college too. Now I remember, Stockdale, a small fellow."*

*"No, they're not from our college."*

*"But what about the grants you give for digging?"*

*"There are no grants, as you term them."*

*"Are you sure? I mean—"*

*"Not at Dartmoor. I should know. I'm chair for that department. No, no, nothing going on there for sure. And as for those names, perhaps you have the colleges mixed up. But I pretty well know all the other chaps in that field around here and I should recognize their names. Maybe you heard them wrong. Of course it could have been Oxford or one of the other colleges."*

*"And you say there is no funding at all for Dartmoor?"*

*"None. What is this all about? Does it have something to do about the tragedies in Devon?"*

*"I don't know. I don't know for sure, but thank you."*

"Doc, my mind was buzzing like a bunch of killer bees as I left the cafe. The morning bells were peeling all through the town as

I found a park bench. *Who were those guys?* The professor was certainly knowledgeable enough. But I was sure he said King's College. Why would he say that if it wasn't true? Something was snapping like a continuous rubber band in my head, Doc. That cop hunter instinct was making my already-high blood pressure surge. I could feel it pulsating inside me. *What the hell was going on? And who was that Latimer? And that quiet guy named Spensor who never said anything whenever I saw them together?* Something was wrong, Doc. I knew something was rotten."

# Chapter 15

"When I returned to my room I called the Exeter Police station, and after pleading with the desk sergeant that I had information on the dog attacks, I got Sergeant Hopkins' home phone number."

*"Hello?"* It was a young woman's voice.

*"Is Sergeant Hopkins in please?"*

*"Yes, just a minute please."* I could hear her calling the young sergeant.

*"Yes? Can I help you?"*

*"Stanley, this is Bill Hughes. Remember the New York cop at the inn?"*

*"Of course, Mr. Hughes. What can I do for you? I guess you heard we had another attack the other day. Old man Ferguson got it. Even ate his dog too. Boy, the Chief Inspector is going crazy and is taking it out on us chaps for sure."*

*"Yes, I can well imagine. Stanley, I may or may not have something for you. I came across it by accident. But I want you to hear it first. You know what I mean, to see what you think? Then perhaps the inspector would listen if we both approached him."*

*"Go on, Mr. Hughes—sounds interesting."*

"Doc, I related the whole cafe story to the young policeman.

*"Well, what do you think?"*

*"Damn well may be something to it, Mr. Hughes."*

*"Call me Bill, Stanley."*

*"I tell you what, Bill. It would go over better if you, as an experienced homicide officer, explained the information to the inspector. Of course I'll be with you. He doesn't cater to underling opinions. Could you find a way to come down again?"*

*"Yes, I'll come. But I think I need to stay at Princetown. If these guys are the suspects, they may get suspicious if I turn back up there at the inn."*

"Doc, Princetown, as I mentioned before, was just a little way down the road from Postbridge. But ironically, I was more apprehensive about asking for leave from the administrators than anything.

*"Gentlemen, that's correct. I need a small leave of absence."*

"The two academics sat snug in their heavy leather chairs peeping over their bifocals.

*"But Mr. Hughes, you've only been back a few weeks?"*

*"Yes, I know sir—but this is of paramount importance. In fact, as an old policeman's adage, it could be 'a matter of life and death' to be honest."*

*"Good heavens! Has it anything to do with that Dartmoor matter that you happened to encounter while visiting there, by chance?"*

*"Yes, sir—I think I can be of assistance to the police."*

*"Oh, then by all means go, sir."*

*"Thank you, gentlemen."*

*"Of course you'll inform us of the situation when you return?"*

*"Yes, sir, and to the minute detail. Thank you."*

"It was three days later when I boarded the train. The ride was awful, Doc. For some reason the cars were awfully crowded. Sergeant Hopkins picked me up at the Exeter station. It was dark as we rode toward the Princetown Hotel and all the while we discussed the cafe incident at Cambridge.

*"It's amazing what you learned, Bill."*

*"You know what I have a gut feeling about, Stanley?"*

*"What's that?"*

*"I think they found something. I remember the professor saying how there were lost mine shafts and tunnels all over the place. It just might have something to do with how those farms are laid out."*

"The next day, Doc, I got a map and pinned it on the wall of my hotel room. Somehow Sergeant Hopkins had persuaded the chief inspector to listen to my hypothesis. We sat in my small Princetown room with the aroma of hot tea permeating the interior. I began.

*"Now Chief Inspector, I know I'm intruding, and I used to hate like hell when some guy would jump on my cases, but I really believe you're about to have another killing very shortly."*

*"Thank you, Mr. Hughes. To be honest, I'm about at the end of it. I apologize if I had seemed offensive before, but as you say, it was the outside thing. I can tell you here in front of Hopkins that we are pulling our hair out and everyone is short tempered at the department. The pressure is overwhelming from London. I'll listen, and most gratefully, if you believe you have come across anything that can help us. Please go ahead."*

"The inspector was now humbled by the whole horrifying course of events, Doc. Hell, I didn't even know if what I had was real, but I was suddenly thrown back to my old office and going over a murder situation. I went into the case, Doc—I was in my element and presented my summation.

*"As I mentioned before, when I checked around Cambridge and found out that these guys weren't associated with any of the colleges, I felt that cop hunter instinct. As I told Hopkins on the way here last night, those guys were lying, Inspector. And when the professor took me out for a look around the moors, he may have told me more than he meant to. I mean, I may be barking up the wrong tree, but perhaps—just perhaps—this could be what they're up to. Professor Latimer said that in the old folklore tales there were old, covered mine shafts and tunnels all over the place. Then he said that during the road bandit period, if I'm not mistaken—I think you call them highwaymen here in England—that these old tunnels were stashing places for the stolen goods. He went on to explain that the legends say there may still be treasure worth millions in one of those tunnels. So, what if he has found something—say a map—or stumbled on something in a dig or whatever, enough to cause them to kill for the ultimate goal? What if the professor and his guys are after the area where those farms are located but can't get there because it'll cause a ruckus?"*

*"Maybe so, maybe so. But what does that have to do with the dog attacks? Couldn't he have just struck up a deal with the farmers?"*

*"I just don't know that answer, Inspector."*

The inspector turned to the sergeant, *"Have they sold the Johnson farm yet?"*

*"Yes, sir, I checked into it. 'Twas last week."*

*"Well, check out who purchased it—that seems like an extremely quick sale. And what about Ferguson's farm? Is it up for sale?"*

144

"Yes, sir."

"Maybe, Bill Hughes, you may be on to something."
The inspector brought the tea cup up to his lips.

"But why don't we just twist one of them, sir— squeeze 'em a little?" inquired the sergeant.

"Can't do that, son. We'll never get them."

"The inspector is right, Stanley. They'll fly the coop."

The inspector rubbed his thinning hair, "But what about those damn dogs? How could they have used them? And where are they hidden?"

"I don't know. When I visited the site they only had one cur and he was certainly no pack hound or attack dog. I'm just not sure—or even if it's them. But they have lied, and that is at least something to stand on."

"You're right."

"Now, let me show you this map I have pinned on the wall. See how the farmhouses are laid out? Now I'll draw a line to each one of the farms and—"

"Damn, it's almost a perfect triangle!"

"Yes, Inspector, that got to me too, but I'm not sure what it means. However, two of the farmers on the triangle point are dead."

"Doc, a quiet calm came over the whole room and we just sat there staring at the chart lines. I finally broke the silence.

"You know what has set in my mind? Something is going to happen to farmer Morse Hudson. That triangle tells me so. I just bet he's next on the list for whatever reason."

Sergeant Hopkins quickly answered, "Oh, I saw him here at the inn just the other day. His missus wants out and he seems so scared lately. I think he's ready to sell."

"I can understand."

145

*"What do you mean Mr. Hughes?"* asked the inspector.

*"He saw what I saw. I know you think I'm out of my mind on that devil hound thing, but he saw it too."*

*"How do you know?"*

*"He told me."*

*"My God, come on, Mr. Hughes, you're a professional—those things just don't exist."*

*"Well, he called me to his place and that's when he told me. But hound or no hound, Mr. Hudson is going to be the next victim—it's in my bones, Inspector."*

*"Yes, yes, I understand. It's just all so confusing. Those men...and some hound. It's beyond any reason. This is a damned nightmare."*

"Again we were quiet, Doc. Then it came to me like a lightning bolt. Do what Sherlock Holmes did in *The Hound of the Baskervilles*. Put the bait out! Get the killer to strike and be waiting for him.

*"I have it!"*

*"What?"*

*"We'll get Hudson to be the guinea pig. We'll set him up for an easy hit and be waiting for the attack if it should come."*

*"All well and good, but he's so scared as it is right now, I don't think he'd agree to anything, Mr. Hughes."*

*"Yes I know, Stanley, but I think I can talk to him— we are, as I mentioned, somewhat kin on an event from hell."*

*"But do you think that if it is these men that they'll take the chance to strike again? I mean it seems like they would want to wait a spell so that the heat is off. Or what if Hudson just decides to sell?"*

146

"That's a good point, Stanley, but I believe that time is running out on them if it is these guys. They've already been out there months and months. Eventually a newspaper or somebody inquisitive will start asking questions and they'll have to answer questions that can be traced. He knows that I'm at Cambridge. No, I feel that they need to move quickly to see if they can get the prize. Whatever that may be."

"Yes, good, very good. We'll check who's purchased the Johnson farm and see if someone's interested in Ferguson's place also. I'll call you tomorrow, Mr. Hughes. Then we can get back together. God, I hope this is the answer. I haven't slept in what feels like a year. This damn Dartmoor does seem like it's Satan's playground." The inspector finished off his tea.

"Doc, when they left the room I felt better than I had in a long while, but being on the moors again brought back Jenny in an awfully bad way. And I also thought about the night that almost drove me stark raving mad. What in the hell did I really see? Had the LSD and booze petrified my brain cells? But then again, what about old man Hudson? He saw it too, but he had been taking in the pints that night at the inn's pub. It was all a maddening, twisting jumble."

"That's understandable."

"Well, the next day, Doc, Sergeant Hopkins picked me up and we drove to Exeter. The chief inspector had learned that a guy named Morrison from London had bought the Johnson farm. But the surprise was that the same real estate firm had made an inquiry on the Fergusons' farm within days of the demise of Mr. Ferguson. To the inspector things were greatly looking up.

"Do you think that Mr. Hudson will assist us, Mr. Hughes?"

"I don't know, but if it's handled right maybe we

147

can get his help. *Let me talk to him alone. I think he really trusts me since we had the same encounter.*"

"Doc, I don't mean to deviate from the story, but probably one of the strangest events of all happened the next day—it really unsettled me. It was a Sunday morning and I had planned to eat a leisurely breakfast at the Princetown Hotel. I had just come down the stairs and seated myself in the small dining room when I noticed a young child staring at me from the clerk's counter. She held a tiny doll, Doc, and never took her eyes off of me. She was maybe five or six years old or something like that. I had ordered my meal, and when I looked up she was still looking at me. It was uncanny, Doc. For some reason it made me a bit nervous. It was as if she was reading me. When the proprietor came in with my breakfast I asked him who the little girl was.

*"Oh, she's my youngest child, sir."*

*"Well, she's awfully quiet and just seems to have a fascination about me."*

*"Dear me, I'm sorry—she must be staring at you. She does that with certain people."*

*"Well, you should be proud. She's a lovely princess for sure."*

*"That she is, sir. She's my angel for sure. She had a bad accident about a year ago and my poor darling hasn't said a word since."*

*"Oh, I'm sorry."*

*"Oh, that's all right, sir. She was playing with her friends late in the afternoon and near dusk she went after her puppy that had run away. See that tor over on the top of yonder hill?"*

"I looked out the window to the bluish and umber mound that lay not a mile away.

*"She was never to go that far, but she did it anyway.*

*All we know is that when her friends found her behind one of the stones that her puppy was missing and she was standing like she was frozen. No crying, no nothing, and my little angel has never spoken another word since that day. We think one of the sheepdogs that was loose got the pup and scared her. The doctors said she had a seizure and ever since that day she stays around the inn. If she's making you feel uneasy, I'll get her in the kitchen, sir."*

*"No, no, on the contrary, ask her if she'll come sit with me. I think she's looking at me for a reason and I'd like to know why. She's such a charmer."*

*"Very well, sir. Like I said, she does that from time to time. I'll see if she would like to sit with you—will you be needing anything else, sir?"*

*"No. I'm fine, thank you."*

"I watched the father talk to the child, Doc. She never said anything back, just nodded. Then, as little shy girls do, she ever so slowly advanced to the side of my table. Her father was watching as she came up to the table. Then he approached.

*"What's her name?"*

*"Annie, sir. She won't answer you, but she knows her name is Annie."*

"The owner then left us and disappeared behind the kitchen door.

*"Hello, Annie."*

"She never took her eyes off of me. I felt so uneasy. But then I knew. Together we knew. We both looked at each other for a few moments. Doc, it was an invisible and soundless bonding of spirits.

*"Annie, you saw the big doggie didn't you? You saw the big dog hurting your puppy and you know by some reason that I have seen it too. That's why you're staring at me aren't you, Annie?"*

149

"Doc, as God is my witness, I watched the tiniest tear in the whole world come from her eye. She wanted to talk. Her mouth opened, but nothing came out. But more than that, I noted on her right arm a long, reddish, elongated mark that ran from her hand to her elbow. It looked like a healed burn.

*"You saw it, Annie. And nobody would believe you, would they?"*

"Another tear rolled down her cheek, Doc.

*"But you're right, Annie, I saw him too—only us who have seen him know, don't we?"*

"She didn't nod or anything but brought the small doll she had up to her cheek.

*"It's okay, my sweet darling. I love you because you and I are so together. We just know about the secret, don't we? I understand...I understand."*

"Doc, that child came and cuddled next to me. Thank God we were alone because I felt the tears she had shown coming into my eyes. For a few moments she was my child—sounds corny, but I felt we were something like father and daughter. She was so gentle and yet had been shattered by that damned incident. How can evil be allowed to assault a child, Doc? In all my years on the force I still question what is called God's infinite wisdom and love whenever I see a child destroyed by any type of malignancy."

"Go on, Bill."

"She finally just meandered away and went through the door her father had previously entered, and suddenly I didn't feel so alone in my anxiety. I reasoned that there was Constable Clayton, myself, Farmer Hudson, and now Annie who had seen the damn thing.

"To be honest I just never went to sleep that night. All that happened to Jenny, the killings, and now the child—hell, I was all screwed up. So I just downed about five glasses of scotch and crashed."

# Chapter 16

"The next day I rode a bike to Hudson's house. It was farther than I thought from Princetown. It was warmer than usual, but it was still a typical British steel gray day. I noted Hudson had obtained two new dogs as I peddled up to the gate. He was just coming from behind the house when he saw me. He eyed me warily until he recognized me and gave me a wave to come on into the yard.

*"Good to see you, Bill."*

*"Same here, Morse. I was sorry to hear about Mr. Ferguson."*

*"Yes, he was my best drinking mate, as was Sidney Johnson. How we loved our pints at the pub...now look at us around the moor. We're literally under attack and the authorities are absolutely useless. My wife wants out, and now I'm beginning to see her way of things. She's gone to live with our daughter in Plymouth. Too many weird things about now, Bill. I can't even sleep at all anymore. But by God, this was me grandfather's and me father's—I just want to hold on so bad, don't you know?"*

*"Of course. Heard any more howls?"*

*"Oh yeah, maybe about a week ago. Sent chills into these old bones, I'll tell you for sure. To be honest, I think I've become paranoid. But how are you?"*

*"Okay I guess. Now that we are sort of brothers in what we saw, I thought I'd come down and see if perhaps*

*you'd like to listen to a theory I have about all this."*

*"Of course, let's go in for some tea."*

"As we sat down, I let the old man release his feelings on the latest events as I had been trained to do in the department. Finally he had settled down. Then he stood up, went over to a small bookshelf, pulled out a worn book, and came back and sat at the table.

*"I want to read you something, Bill. Just keep an open mind if you will and hear me out, then I'll listen to what you have to say."*

*"Sure, please go on."*

*"I'm going to read what was said in the Baskerville story. I read it just the other night—hadn't read the old Holmes story since I was a wee lad. But hear me out on this one part please."*

*"I'm with you."*

*"I'm on the part when Dr. Mortimer was reading the legendary Baskerville manuscript to Sherlock Holmes and Dr. Watson. I won't read it all, but just this part when the drunken revelers were with Hugo Baskerville that night and followed him as he pursued the innocent farm girl. I'm sure you recall the chaps were behind Sir Hugo on horseback as he tried to catch her for his lustful pleasure. They had just ridden up to a small ravine."*

*"Please go on. I'm listening, Morse."*

"The old man brought the book up close to his bifocals.

*" 'The company had come to a halt, more sober men, as you may guess, than when they started. Most of them would by no means advance, but three of them, the boldest, or it may be the most drunken, rode forward down the goyal. Now, it opened into a broad space in which stood two of those great stones, still to be seen there, which were set by certain forgotten peoples in the days of old. The moon was*

*shining bright upon the clearing, and there in the centre lay the unhappy maid where she had fallen, dead of fear and fatigue. But it was not the sight of her body, nor yet was it that of the body of Hugo Baskerville lying near her, which raised the hair upon the heads of these daredevil roysterers, but it was that, standing over Hugo, and plucking at his throat, there stood a foul thing, a great, black beast, shaped like a hound, yet larger than any hound that ever mortal eye has rested upon. And even as they looked the thing tore the throat out of Hugo Baskerville, on which, as it turned its blazing eyes and dripping jaws upon them, the three shrieked with fear and rode for dear life, still screaming, across the moor. One, it is said, died that very night of what he had seen, and the other twain were but broken men for the rest of their days.'"*

"He laid the book on a table and removed his glasses.

*"What I'm getting at, Bill, is that we might fall right in with the story. I mean that Constable Clayton is now near death's door, and you and I are messed up, there's no denying that. It all fits with the story. Something happens to those who see that apparition or whatever it is. Our minds are whirling, Bill. The legend said that the ones who saw it were broken men for the rest of their days."*

*"Yes, I see what you're getting at."*

*"Whoever sees it is somewhat doomed, Bill. At least I'm beginning to feel that way."*

*"Yes. I saw a small child this weekend who I think saw it awhile back."*

*"Oh, ya mean the little girl at the hotel in Princetown?"*

*"Then you know of her?"*

*"Oh yes, but I thought she was just a mentally ill*

child. What makes you think she saw what we saw?"

"I know, I just know. She cried when I asked her. She can't speak, but she knew I had seen it too."

"My God in heaven, that sweet child!"

"Yes. We'll need God awfully bad before this is all over."

"Who?"

"God."

"Right you are, Bill. I'm afraid for all of us."

"Mind if I smoke, Morse?"

"Oh, no sir...please accommodate yourself and I'll light me pipe."

"Hudson and I became somewhat still and stared into the small fire that was barely alive in the coal hearth.

"I wonder if we'll both go daft before it's over. I mean there seems to be no rest at night, and all I do is look over my shoulder all day. I never even so much as let the dogs out at night anymore."

"If you have some time, Morse, I'd like to relate some events that have recently happened. I know it's not all the answers, but here it goes anyway."

"Please do, sir."

"Doc, I explained the whole scenario to the Dartmoor man, and he never so much as moved in his chair.

"Sweet Jesus, those guys who we see at the pub in the evenings, eh?"

"Please understand, it's not for certain that they are the problem. But something's not right with them. So Morse, that's where I was hoping you might help us. By us I mean your police."

"But how does it involve me?"

"Again I went over the meager evidence and unfolded the

map showing the triangle. His cottage was the last point in completing the pyramid of the geometric lines.

*"Oh, Lord! Then they'll be after me you think?"*

*"Maybe, just maybe. Again I'm just theorizing, but we could find out for sure if you'll help us."*

*"But what of that damned hound? Where do they keep him if it's them causing all the problems? And for that fact, I can't believe what I saw was any dog of this earth!"*

*"I don't know. I just don't know for sure."*

*"Do ya think they have hidden a pack of dogs that could have attacked Johnson and Ferguson?"*

*"I don't know that either."*

*"I see."*

"I could tell he became dejected.

*"We just have to lure them out if it's their aim to get you."*

*"I grasp the situation, Bill. But in my heart I don't feel that's what happened to me. It went to the core of me soul, Bill. It was not a manmade fright. My heart was almost bursting from the fear of what I felt and saw with me own eyes."*

*"I know, but damn it, we've got to be rational. Someone has to be behind it. Someone must be—or indeed we are both 'ruined' as you just read."*

*"Then for my peace of mind and my very well-being I must go with you. Is that what you're saying, Bill?"*

*"Yes. You and I have to see if this is the answer. We must if we are to make any reasonable sense of this whole nightmare. Our sanity is at stake, Morse."*

*"Then tell me what to do."*

"Doc, the next day Sergeant Hopkins picked Mr. Hudson and me up at the Princetown Hotel and we drove over to the police station in Exeter. There was a large blackboard on the inspector's wall. I recognized the chalk lines immediately. He'd drawn out the road that led from Postbridge to Morse Hudson's farm. As we sat down around a table he introduced us to four other officers who were seated. The meeting began quickly.

*"Now gentlemen, Mr. Hudson will go to The Red Bull inn and pub tomorrow night in a normal fashion. Wednesday nights I believe are your standard evenings, is that correct, sir?"*

"Hudson nodded his head in agreement.

*"Then please park your lorry in front of the inn but at the side where the trees give a bit of cover. I want your lorry to be seen from the road. If these are our villains, I want them to be assured you're in the pub. If they don't show up, then we'll just have to try again. The other officers here will be in plain cars and will drop Sergeant Hopkins and I off down the road a piece. Then we'll walk to the inn, get into the back of your truck, and hide. When you leave—"*

*"Wait, sir."*

*"Yes, Mr. Hudson?"*

*"Isn't Mr. Hughes going to be with you?"*

*"Well, I didn't want to endanger him, Mr. Hudson."*

*"But sir, I'd feel more comfortable if he was in the back of the lorry too. There's more than enough room, sir. Besides we both have something in common we'd like to see finished so to speak."*

*"Very well. I'll catch hell if headquarters finds out, so it does not go beyond this door, understood? Mr. Hughes, would you feel like a cold night's ride?"*

*"Certainly, anything for Mr. Hudson."*

*"Good. Then we'll have the lads here drop us off, as I said, down the road and we'll climb into the lorry. It's*

*darker on the side of the inn, I'm sure no one will see us. You'll note here on the board that I have the road broken down into one-quarter miles. Mr. Hudson, every time your odometer hits a quarter of a mile, you let me know through the sliding back window if you will. I will have my handheld radio and will inform the backup officers where we are as we progress toward your farm. So you men keep a sharp ear on the radio."*

The other officers answered in a military, *"Yes, sir."*

*"These men, Mr. Hudson, as I said, will be in plain dress and in unmarked cars. They'll be parked about two miles away on the main road to Princetown, so we'll have ample reinforcements for your safety.*

*"Now, Mr. Hudson, when you go in the pub, let those fellows hear as you talk to the others around the bar that your wife is gone out of town and you can stay for a few extra pints. That will put you leaving a little later than normal. I think they will leave earlier than you, so wait awhile before leaving. That will give them time to form their plan to do whatever they do to stop you or follow you. Hopkins, be sure and bring your firearm and I'll have mine. You other men do the same. I'm not sure what we'll meet out there. They could have a pack of dogs with them."*

*"Yes, sir, I'll have it ready."*

"Doc, Mr. Hudson looked at me like a piece of cold ice, almost helplessly, as if resigned that he was nothing but bait. We both hoped to God that this would end our purgatory.

*"Well, gentlemen, any questions?"*

No one answered.

*"Very well. Hopefully after tomorrow evening this will bring an end to this infernal investigation. You men are dismissed."*

157

"The other uniformed policemen acknowledged his command and immediately left the room. Only Stanley Hopkins, Mr. Hudson, and I remained seated.

"*I would appreciate it if Mr. Hughes and Mr. Hudson would stay a moment. Stanley, please bring the car around and we'll be out shortly.*"

"*Yes, sir.*"

"*Now I can become a human and not a commander to you two. Mr. Hughes, you know what I mean. I just want to thank you both from the bottom of my heart and from an old worn-out policeman. Even if this doesn't work out, I want you to know that I am most grateful for your valuable assistance. Let's all say a prayer that this is the end.*"

"He was really a changed man, Doc. As these events had changed me, Constable Clayton, that little girl, and Mr. Hudson...I could see that they had even affected the inspector.

"Even though Jenny was lost, for the first time since I had arrived back at Dartmoor my spirits seemed to rise a bit. I had an anticipation that things were coming to a reasonable ending and—as Sherlock Holmes had said so many times—'the game's afoot!'

"*Let's have a bite to eat, Mr. Hughes, then we'll come back and start again. You need the time to collect your thoughts and just to refresh.*"

"*Thank you, Inspector.*"

"It was fish and chips plus tea, compliments of the inspector.

"*Now that we're all full, Mr. Hughes, sit down and we'll start again. But don't doze off on me after a meal now.*"

"*Yeah, okay.*"

"They took me back to the hotel, and the next morning I noticed the small child didn't come back out of the kitchen. I reasoned her father thought that she was a bother to me. But just as I

158

took my first sip of coffee, I saw her through the large dining room window. She was standing next to a rusty swing with her doll and staring as if transfixed toward the tor that her father had pointed out to me. What in God's name was going through her mind? And if Hudson and I were having problems coping with that vision of hellish horror, how was she able to stand the mental pain?

"I pretty well stayed around the small town that day, just walking, going back and forth, missing Jenny, and suddenly having doubts about condemning the archeologist professor—if they were archeologists. Maybe I was all wrong. Perhaps he just wanted his privacy and told me about Cambridge as a way to satisfy my curiosity and meddling. Around six o'clock that evening two constables picked me up at the hotel. I was a nervous wreck, Doc, I can tell you that for sure."

# Chapter 17

"Who wouldn't be, Bill? Do go on."

"Well, it must have been about seven o'clock or a little later when Inspector Martin, Sergeant Hopkins, and I were let off just around the curve from Postbridge. It had gotten downright chilly again and a light mist or fog was passing above us. All of us were in heavy foul weather coats. The Red Bull Inn was lit up, and we saw that Mr. Hudson had followed the inspector's instructions as his lorry was parked on the darker side of the parking lot. I looked around the parking lot and said a few profanities as the archeologist's Land Rover was nowhere to be seen. We quietly climbed over the tailgate and shut the canvas cover. We were much relieved when we saw the old farmer had even put some blankets inside for us. And we used them too, Doc."

"Yes, go on."

"I mean no sooner had we gotten inside the back of the truck than we heard a vehicle rumble into the parking lot with its headlights streaming through the canvas. Then came the slow crunch and crackle of the gravel as it pulled almost next to us. Of all the damn luck, Doc, it was them—a few minutes earlier and they would have seen us! We didn't even breathe as we heard their voices. The inspector pressed his finger to his lips for silence as the doors were opening and slamming.

*"That's Hudson's lorry all right."*

"That was the end of their conversation so far as we could hear, but they were still conversing as they entered the inn. We wanted to catch more of their conversation but their footsteps in the pebbles drowned that hope.

"Doc, it got miserable in the back of that truck. The others had gloves but I had forgotten mine. Just after the suspects entered, the inspector did a radio check on his handheld mobile to the backup crew that was down the road.

*"Loud and clear, sir,"* the report came back.

*"Now boys, don't call me back. Stay off the radio. I don't want anything coming through here until I call you."*

The radio crackled back, *"We copy you, Inspector. Over."*

"I would guess maybe an hour had passed as the chill deepened and penetrated inside that lorry.

*"What time is it?"*

*"Eight-thirty, sir."*

"Then a door opened and some unknown men left the inn. Cranked up their vehicle and roared off.

"It was so bitter, Doc, I remember I couldn't blow on my hands anymore. Once more the inn door opened, and again more voices. Footsteps could be heard and the doors to the Range Rover opening and shutting. The vehicle's lights again illuminated the back of the truck and then the engine started. The yellow beams slowly disappeared as the Rover backed away. With a roar it left us in silence again. They were gone.

*"Thank God, I'm almost an ice cream stick."* Poor Hopkins was shaking and gritting his teeth.

*"Are you okay, Mr. Hughes?"*

*"Yes, thank you, Inspector, but my toes are numb."*

*"I guess we all should have dressed warmer, but I want Hudson to wait awhile before he comes out, so hold on chaps, a bit longer."*

*"I have to winkie so bad."*

161

*"Damn you, Hopkins, I told you to go before we came out."*

*"I did, Inspector, but I'm hurting."*

*"Hold it, damn it. You can't get out. They may be just a few yards from here watching the parking lot."*

*"Yes, sir."*

"Finally it was about nine o'clock when Hudson came out. He was talking with some other fellows and we heard their car doors slam and the motor start. Finally the lorry door opened and the back cab window slid open.

*"Are you boys frozen out now?"*

*"Yes, quite chilled, Mr. Hudson."*

*"Here then, I keep a bit under my seat here for such nights. It'll warm you up, lads."*

"He passed a bottle through the opening, and on duty or not on duty, we each gulped a swallow from the bottle, Doc. It burned so good as it went down.

*"Okay, Mr. Hudson let's get going. Don't speed or go too slow. Just drive like you normally would. And oh yes, would you unscrew or turn off your interior light please? Shan't want them to spot us if you open your door."*

*"Right you are, Inspector."*

"We all looked at each other, Doc, and we immediately knew the farmer was feeling no pain, much less the frozen air. As we rolled out of the driveway the inspector called the other cars to inform them that we were on the move.

*"Sergeant, you'd better unstrap that back canvas a bit so we can make a quick exit. Just hold it down so it won't flip up should they come up from behind us."*

*"Yes, sir."*

"I was absolutely frozen with cold, Doc.

*"Mr. Hudson, could you keep this window open all*

162

*the way so that we can get some heat back here please?"*

*"No problem, Mr. Hughes."*

*"Here's the end of the first quarter mile coming up, Inspector."*

"The inspector called the backup cars again.

*"We've passed the second quarter. Don't start out yet. Wait till I give the word. Don't move."*

"The road was shaky and rolling, and even in our prone-like position we tossed and bounced as we kept trying to keep our balance, and all the while the loose tools rattled and clanked in rhythm. I could see Hopkins' breath as we attempted to keep some kind of equilibrium. Farmer Hudson all the while was whistling. I wasn't sure if it was his way of controlling his fear or the dumping down of pint after pint.

*"Man oh man, do I have to whiz."*

*"Cut the crap, Hopkins. Thank God we have a nice crack here in the canvas so I can see the front. I can see just ahead, but the damnable fog is setting in."* The inspector was suddenly intense, *"I don't want to look through the cab window. I could be reflected should they be ahead of us somewhere."*

*"Another quarter, Inspector."*

"It went on that way, Doc, for a while, and when I looked out the canvas on my side, the front lorry lights seemed to mirror off the mists that wrapped around the old truck. The vehicle's beams just made a glow instead of an illuminated path.

*"Another quarter, Inspector."*

"It must have been when we were at the twelfth quarter that Mr. Hudson changed his soft tone.

*"There's some blinking lights ahead, Inspector. What do you want me to do?"*

*"Slow down now, Mr. Hudson. Sergeant get ready."*

*"Yes, sir."*

"He then called the other cars and gave them the quarter mile number.

*"We're at the twelfth quarter of the mile mark—be ready to come fast when I call you."*

The inspector's radio squeaked back, *"Roger, three miles, sir."*

*"I'm almost there, Inspector."*

*"That's okay, Mr. Hudson, just nice and slow now."*

"I could see through the break in the stiff fabric a dull red flashing ahead, and as I turned I saw the inspector pull out his gun.

*"Ready Hopkins?"*

*"Ready, sir."*

"Hopkins had his weapon pointed toward the truck bed.

*"It's a white car or something and someone's waving in the center of the road, Inspector."*

*"Okay, just come to a stop and don't let on we're back here—just try to be normal, Mr. Hudson."*

*"I'm okay... It's them! The Land Rover is on the side of the road and the professor is waving his arms."*

*"Okay, pull to a stop, Mr. Hudson."*

*"Tally ho, Inspector, here we go!"* The farmer's voice was almost humorous.

"As we came to a squeaking halt, Hudson rolled down his window.

*"Thank God you came by, Mr. Hudson. I'm not sure, but we may have busted an axle or something. None of us are that great of a mechanic. Maybe you can tell? I hate to impose on you on such a nasty night."*

*"No problem, sir."*

*"We may need a lift if you don't mind. Perhaps you could help us and take a look. Barney and John are trying to*

*check it out."*

*"Of course, be glad to look her over. Let me get me torch."*

"The door slammed, and I, as well as Inspector Martin, watched through the canvas crack. The old farmer walked to the front of the Land Rover. The two men in front of the vehicle then stood up.

"Doc, it was like a split second and all hell broke loose.

*"What the bloody hell?!"* Hudson's voice was a shout.

*"Don't move, Mr. Hudson, or I'll have to shoot you."*

*"What the hell are you doing? Robbing me?"*

*"John, hand me the rod please."*

"There was a terrific yell from the old farmer.

*"That's it—let's go!"* blurted the inspector.

"The young sergeant jumped from the truck followed by the inspector and me. Suddenly an agonizing cry echoed from the front of the Land Rover. Just as we came in view of the professor and the other men, we saw old Mr. Hudson go down.

*"Hold it! Police!"*

"A combination shot and flash came from the muscular man and the inspector and Hopkins returned the fire. The gunman went down.

*"Don't shoot for God's sake! Don't shoot! I'm not armed!"*

"The smaller man held his hands straight up. As he reached upward he let go of a rope, which was tied to the old dog that I had seen at the professor's camp. The terrified animal took off running.

*"Watch it! There goes the professor. He's off!"*

*"I'll watch this one. Hopkins, go get the bastard."*

*"I can't sir, I'm shot."*

165

*"What?"*

*"My arm sir, it's me arm."*

My response was almost involuntary, *"I'll get him."*

"Doc, I was my old police self again. As the suspect disappeared into the mists, I could hear the inspector literally screaming for the backup cars on his handheld walkie-talkie while I began the chase.

*"Get Hopkins' gun, Hughes!"*

"I stopped dead in my tracks and behind me was Hopkins trying to keep up.

*"I can't make it, sir—here take my gun."*

*"Go back, Stanley."*

"I was flying across the path that seemed to be heading uphill, but I was breathing so heavily that I had to stop. I cussed at there being only a half moon. Just further up the knoll I could make out the professor still putting distance between us. I was losing him. Then we both went down a gully and back up a small bluff. Now I was out of sight of the Land Rover and Hudson's lorry. It was just me and the professor. Suddenly we were just two lone figures on the dark abominable moor. God, I felt so helpless—I didn't know where I was, and now I was alone with a killer. Even worse, the terrain was my enemy and his ally. I watched him fall and then I too came to a stop to catch my breath. He got back up and was headed for the tor— you know, the crags that I told you about that sit on top of the hills."

"Yes, I remember."

"He was still gaining distance, and the damn combination of the darkness and the mist that was now swirling around me was making me lose sight of him from time to time. I was at a slow shuffle, to be honest, and had lost him again. I still recall how it seemed like I was a hundred miles from the scene and beyond any help at all should he be armed. Then, damn it, I tripped and it knocked the wind out of me. As I tried to stand, my bad knee buckled.

"Doc, it was the same stone that had tripped him—and there lay his pistol. Now at least I felt better. As I kept on, everything in my body that could beat was thumping like a drum. I was too old for the hunt. When I was almost midway up the hill I quickly looked back. There was nothing—no sign of the police car lights or the scene where the pursuit began. Now it was just me and him in the murky darkness and I was not only thoroughly exhausted but damned well panicky. He was bigger than me—I could never even begin to stand up in a hand-to-hand fight with him as exhausted as I was. But at least I had the gun. He kept moving up the rise where the rocks poked out of the ground like giant gnarled fingers. Still I managed to keep some kind of uncoordinated pace.

"Once more I looked back in desperate hope for any kind of assistance. Now that we were both near the top of the tor, I finally saw some light specks that had to be the scene and the other police cars. But they were like hazy dots—like distant stars. Any help looked like a million miles away. I was almost ready to collapse as I came to the top of the hill where the monstrous stones seemed to come to life—each one protruded from the ground as if pushed up through the earth by some colossal underground god. They were huge and looming. Then...then, I saw...then I saw..."

"Come on now, Bill, you're shaking again. Calm down. Here, take a slow sip of this."

"I'm shaking again, Doc. I'm shaking bad."

"Just breathe deeply."

"It was there. It was there!"

"Go on, get it out."

"Just ahead I saw something large moving near the top of one of those rocks. It was blacker than the night sky behind it. A tinge of reddish glow masked its head. Sweet Mother of God, it was that black thing again! I saw it, Doc, as clear as I see you."

"Easy, Bill, easy."

"It was on a rock ledge and it leaped off—and I saw it land on the professor, Doc! I raised my gun, but I was in such a state of uncontrollable shakes that the pistol was useless in my hands—my trigger finger became soft as the marsh mud. I was totally beyond any self control, and the man's screams coupled with the hellish roars and growls all mixed together like a recurring nightmare. It went on and on, and I found myself yelling as loud as the professor. His shrieks were of unbearable pain. Mine were just because I was looking at something that was beyond the mind's capacity to endure. I lost sight of the inhuman struggle for a few seconds, but for some unknown reason I kept shuffling toward the horror, Doc. The high pitched wails for help were more than I could stand. I was beyond myself, I was going into the abyss, and I couldn't stop. I was being sucked into a merciless gore of unfathomable mauling with the ripping of flesh and bone even invading my ears..."

"Slow down, Bill, damn it. You're going too fast!"

"I rounded a boulder and there it was, just standing there in front of the prone professor. It was as if it was waiting on me. Oh God, Doc, this was no made-up, manmade thing—it was the very thing that drove Clayton into a vegetable and killed the joy out of that child. It was as the old farmer had said about being forever ruined. I was in utter shock and I could only stop and stand. I suddenly began to shiver so much, I felt my pants get wet and felt all the cold sweat release from my body. It was staring at me—those searing, dead eyes. Oh God, those eyes!"

"You have to stop now, Bill."

"No. No, I can't. I see it… it was foul and those teeth were white yet stained red, and something was bubbling and foaming from its mouth. The thing seemed to glow around it—God Almighty, Doc, it was from hell. I couldn't do anything, and even worse, I just let the gun drop from my hands. I began sobbing. Can you believe it? I began crying and bawling uncontrollably. I just was ready to die. I wanted to die. It took the life out of my soul little by little—it was draining the spirit from my being."

"Stop now, Bill. Get a hold of yourself, son."

"Suddenly I saw the professor roll over and groan. Then—as if God would not let this end—the dog turned and stared at me, then moved slowly toward me. It was worse than if it would have attacked. I couldn't move if I wanted to; I was whimpering like a baby. As it came closer the odor was beyond description. The thing smelled of death—of a long dead thing. I had smelled all this before when we used to come across day-old bodies. It moved to within a foot of me, Doc. Its black glowing head was up to my neck. God didn't make animals like that, only Satan. It just stood there making a deep guttural noise and turning its head. Oh, those scarlet eyes! I had to close my eyes—I remember even making some kind of uncontrollable whine. Then the beast went around me and sniffed. I felt the nose bump against me. It was so hot. For some mindless reason I opened my eyes and raised my hands as if to show my palms were empty. Then I put them to my side—I think I wanted to show that I could not fight back or did not even want to. I was surrendering to be killed, Doc. Again I closed my eyes and was outside of reality. It stood there snorting with its growling moan, and then an unbearably hot, vile breath swept over my fingers. All of a sudden a fire seared onto my right hand, and when I opened my eyes it had just licked my hand—"

"Stop. You must stop. You're losing complete control. Stop it!"

"No, please… Please, let me finish. It then yawned its mouth and gave a howl that shook the very earth. It went from the air into the very essence of my being. I felt it wash all the life out of me, Doc. I was nothing—I was alive but as dead as the rocks around me. My hand was burning as if coals had been set on it, and I wasn't sure if I was crying from the fright or the pain. I just gave out and fell to my knees.

"Then I saw the professor put an arm against a rock to support himself and begin to stand. Doc, the dog turned, then lunged at the mangled man, grabbed his shoulder, and shook him like a rag doll. I didn't know the human voice could shriek with such pain and horror. I was just a clay spectator as the poor man screamed out his entire insides. Bits of splattered blood hit my face. Then it dropped him again and stared at me."

"For God's sake, please stop, Bill!"

"The professor's moans were not finished when the dog again grabbed him by his leg and began dragging him on a run. Then they disappeared behind the granite rock. The unnerving shouts for mercy from its victim faded into the cold mists."

"God almighty, stop!"

Silence consumed the doctor's office.

# Chapter 18

"My God," Dr. Hansom repeated himself.

"That's right, Doc, 'my God' are the right words. But you see I lived. That's all that mattered. I lived. I survived a trip to the underworld. Yet now I wonder if I really did survive... I am now dissolving from inside. I don't think I can go on anymore."

"We've got to, Bill, we have no choice. Keep going."

"I don't remember anything after that except that it started to drizzle. They found me and took me back to the hospital in Exeter. I was out of it for three days—total delirium. They said I was a raving maniac. But I came back, Doc, I came back. And here's my mark, Doc. See my hand. It's the same burn as was on the child—it's...it's scarlet red."

"We need a break, Bill. We both do. Let's get a drink. Scotch?"

"You have that in a doctor's office?"

"Yeah, for my own medicinal purposes."

"Thank God you're a real doctor."

"Go in the restroom and freshen up, Bill. I'll mix the medicine."

----------- ----------- -----------

"Now maybe we both feel better. So let's go on, Bill. Stand or sit, whatever makes you comfortable."

"I think I need to get up and move a little."

"Good. Now go on."

"Well, as I said before, I was out of it for a while. Then who comes popping in the hospital room but the inspector and the wounded Sergeant Hopkins.

*"Good to see you feeling better, Mr. Hughes."*

*"Thank you. I think I was run over by a freight train. Good God, Stanley, you were winged. What kind of arm rig is that?"*

*"Yes, sir. Nicked a bone fragment out of me elbow. I feel like they put a horse harness around my arm and shoulder."*

*"I guess you should be thankful."*

*"Oh yes, Mr. Hughes, I was extremely lucky."*

*"What about Hudson?"*

*"Except for the cattle prod shocking, he was unhurt."*

*"Thank God, Sergeant, because he's the one that really took the risk."*

"The inspector broke into the conversation.

*"Well, I think you'll be surprised when you listen to this tape, Bill. I'll leave this telephone number on your table. Call me afterwards. I was going to go through the whole episode personally, but the doctor thought it best you not be subjected to anything that might cause a bout of anxiety. But I smuggled in this recording anyway. Anything you need here at the hospital, just yell out."*

*"Thank you, Inspector."*

"When they left I put the small recorder on the bedside table and punched the button. You mentioned when I called you that I might bring any pertinent things that I feel may be of help to me and you, so I brought the tape and a few letters."

"Good, Bill. Do you mind if we listen to it now? I have a cassette player here if you feel all right about it."

"Sure, Doc, go ahead. I've played it a million times."

"Then I'll start it."

Dr. Hansom went over to a file drawer and pulled out a handheld tape recorder and inserted the tape. He clicked it on and placed it on the arm of the overstuffed chair. The tone quality was as if the speakers were conversing in a cave, and at times the distinct sound of exhaling a cigarette could be recognized.

*"This is the statement and confession of Mr. Barney Stockdale. Time: 9:30 A.M., 2nd April 1982. Present is his attorney Mr. Peter Howe, also in the room are Scotland Yard CID Inspector Horace Cater, Detention Officers Lutz and Fry, and myself, Inspector George Martin."*

It went on through the preliminaries and then the questioning began. Inspector Martin's voice was deep and straightforward.

*"Begin your statement, Mr. Stockdale."*

*"I want to state first that I didn't murder anybody. I was hired by Professor Harold Latimer to dig at Dartmoor. I was later threatened that if I did not take part in the events that I was going to be seen to by Mr. John Spensor. I was hired about four months ago by Mr. Latimer to help him work on Dartmoor. When I arrived at the site he had already had John Spensor there at the camp."*

*"Where did you meet Mr. Latimer?"*

*"At a pub called the Green Toad in London."*

*"What had you been doing before you met Mr. Latimer?"*

*"I had just done a turn for burglary. I was broke."*

*"Very well, go ahead."*

*"He said I could make more money than I could ever dream about, but it was so secret that if I joined, I could never back out. Those were his terms. I gathered that what he meant was once in, never out. And if you did make a run, you would be disposed of sorta like. As I said, he took me to*

173

the site at Dartmoor and there I met John Spensor. He had a long record according to Mr. Latimer and got things done. I didn't want to know too much you see, but that Spensor was an odd mate if you get my meaning. He never said much, just sorta mumbled like. He was a brute and mean as hell. There was also another chap who showed up by the name of Jeremy Dixon. Anyway, Mr. Latimer got us into the trailer one evening and told us that he had discovered something on the moor and that if things worked out we would be fabulously wealthy. But if any one of us, after knowing the facts, took off, then we as group would find him and do what was right."

"What did he mean by 'do what was right'?"

"He meant in no uncertain terms that if any one of us split, the others would find the runner and he'd get fixed."

"By 'fixed' you mean killed?"

"That's right, Inspector."

"And what was Mr. Latimer referring to as to what he had found on the moor?"

"Oil, sir."

"Oil?!"

"Yes, sir. You see, he was a geologist."

"Good Lord. Go on man."

"Seems early in the war years, that some blokes discovered oil in the Sherwood area and he said that oil was also here under our feet."

"What's the Sherwood countryside have to do with Dartmoor?"

"I don't know, Inspector, I'm just telling you what he said to us."

"Okay, carry on, Stockdale. We'll check into the Sherwood part later."

*"He said that a dome—whatever that is—was situated within an area of the farms and he drew something like a circle. The farms were Mr. Johnson's, Mr. Ferguson's, and Mr. Hudson's. He said that it would be almost impossible to get the three men to sell all at once. He had heard that two of the farms had been handed down for generations and it would be hopeless to try to get them to cooperate even for a lease. He had also casually or jokingly mentioned it to Mr. Johnson at the pub that what if oil was ever found on the moor? Well, Mr. Johnson said that if it ever was discovered that he would see to it, as well as the other farmers, that their land would never be ruined by dirty oil rigs, and that he would fight it to the hilt. There was no negotiating as far as he was concerned. Of course, Johnson never put it together, as Latimer was supposed to be a college professor of archeology.*

*"Latimer then knew it was going to be an uphill battle to ever get the locals to agree to anything, so he worked out a scheme to scare them off with that Baskerville hound legend. I really didn't know much about the story except what I had seen at the movies, and I'm sure Spensor was completely ignorant about the tale. We would from time to time go out at night and set up speakers and blast the sound of a dog baying. God knows, he sent us out again and again, but the farmers never seemed to waver. Oh, they complained to Constable Clayton over and over and the poor copper was forever running around the tors. Seemed like Officer Clayton was always stopping by our camp asking if we ever heard anything or saw any dogs. Poor old chap, he was at wits end, he was.*

*"Then one night Latimer sent Jeremy Dixon out with the speakers and he never returned. Early the next morning*

175

*we found the car and equipment, but he was gone. Latimer swore that he would get him, and that we were all in this and no one leaves. Jeremy Dixon just never came back. It was really strange because when he disappeared, his keys were still in the car. Dixon just vanished. The professor was stumped, I can tell you. But what really got to us was we found blood all over the place. It was beyond any reason. We drove his car to Exeter and just left it in a parking lot. We checked on it from time to time and nobody ever picked it up. Later we learned that the police took it away. Latimer was really puzzled about Dixon, and the blood on the loudspeakers was even more a mystery. But all this loudspeaker stuff at night, well, it just didn't work, so Mr. Latimer decided that more drastic steps needed to be taken. When he decided to get Mr. Johnson, I wanted to pull out. Believe me, killing was never my game. He then told me that I would not have to take part, I only had to make myself useful as I was rather small like. I later found out that's why he recruited me—it was because I am smallish and a lightweight type.*

*"He drew a drawing for Spensor to weld together. It was basically a posthole digger, but it had bent teeth-like projections on the end of it, ya see. It looked like two jaws with teeth. I can tell you, it put shivers down my spine. I knew then that I had better get out of there. They caught me trying to pack a few things one evening and Spensor beat the hell out of me. So I knew I was hooked, you see."*

*"So you claim they forced you into the situation."*

*"Exactly."*

*"Go on."*

*"Well, he got hold of one of those stun gun things. He said that it was used for cattle or something and it really*

176

knocked them down. *Spensor, I tell you, was a beast—he seemed to relish in it, Inspector. I was so scared. I saw him try the posthole digger with teeth on a sheep after the stun gun knocked it down. God, it was awful. But Spensor, as I said, was laughing as he chewed the poor animal to pieces with that contraption.*

*"Like I said, Latimer was a perfectionist. He had everything planned to the slightest detail. He had Spensor make a pair of steel footpads that had a huge dog-like impression on the bottom. The foot plates had a soft cloth around the edge so that only the dog print showed. They were fitted over my sock feet, and since I was a lightweight he figured I should walk around the place where dog footprints were to be found. He made me test them out, and damned if it didn't leave a perfect impression. I thought he was crazy until he told us both the entire Baskerville legend and how the dog was supposed to be enormous. Again, I must tell you, Inspector, before I go into the rest of the story, I did not kill anyone."*

*"Duly noted, Mr. Stockdale."*

*"We would nip at The Red Bull pub where most of the locals would go, and he waited for Mr. Johnson to leave one night. We followed him home without the Land Rover lights on and he figured out a good place to catch him. I can tell you that I wanted out bad, but I couldn't leave. I had no transportation and they would have surely caught me."*

*"Go on."*

*"It was another Wednesday night that we waited on him as he drove to his home. I think you know where, so I won't go into that. He had the farmer stop his lorry like he tried on Mr. Hudson. But when Mr. Johnson got out, Spensor grabbed him and Latimer hit him with the stun gun in the*

throat. I was instructed to drive his lorry up the road and turn off a seldom-used farm road. They loaded him into the Land Rover and drove to the spot you found him. Latimer said we couldn't leave shoe prints, so he had us put on heavy socks then tape and wrap plastic around them to keep our feet dry. But I can tell you it was extremely cold. It about froze me feet it did. But all we left were just indentures on the ground. Latimer kept insisting that no lights be shown but just his small flashlight."

"Was Mr. Johnson already dead when you arrived at the scene?"

"No, sir. I remember he was groaning when we got to the location. Spensor pulled the farmer out of the Rover and Latimer hit him with the stun gun so much that he was almost dead. Then Spensor went to work on him."

"You mean he wasn't dead when Spensor dug into him with the claws?"

"It was horrible, Inspector. But Latimer said Mr. Johnson had to be alive or the heart wouldn't pump the blood out—he said a dead man doesn't bleed as much, and the whole idea was that he was supposed to be attacked by the hound. I almost ran, but they both had guns and I would have been a dead man."

"Yes. Then what happened?"

"You see, where the stun gun hit him, Spensor made sure that the claw posthole digger would destroy that red mark. I couldn't watch as Spensor dug those things into the farmer's body and throat. Then he chopped up his hands as if he was fighting off the dog bites. Like I said, it was awful— I almost threw up, but Latimer said he would shoot me if I left evidence at the scene. They then got some portable water tanks on their backs and sprayed the area so wet that most of

178

our plastic-covered footprints became just round holes, I was then told to strap on the steel shoe prints and make the dog footprints around the body and a little farther out on the drier soil. Again I'm small, so the imprints wouldn't be so deep. I swear to you, Inspector, I didn't want any part of this. I swear."

"So that's why the ground was always damp? Okay, Mr. Stockdale, go on."

"As we backed the Land Rover out, Spensor lightly broomed our tire tracks then sprayed water over the broom marks. He left the tire tracks of Johnson's lorry so it would look like no other vehicle was involved. Oh yes, he also turned the lorry lights on too. Finally we were out of there. It was basically the same thing for Mr. Ferguson too. But I did not do any of the killing."

"And so when the attack on Mr. Ferguson happened behind his home, they also did his dog in to look like some wild dogs or dog got him?"

"Yes, sir. Mr. Ferguson's dog tried to attack Professor Latimer and he stunned the dog too."

"But how was it that we found real dog hairs and animal saliva at both scenes?"

"Professor Latimer, like I said, had it all down to a tee. He had our dig site guard dog in the Land Rover and made it lick the dead men's face area and hands. And the dog's footprints mixed with my impressed dog prints around the body were just an added feature. I'm sure you've seen the guard dog—he's not big, just a mixed breed, but he slobbers a lot, so that's how it probably got on the clothes. Latimer also cut the dog's hair and sprinkled it on the farmer's clothes. Spensor was all the while laughing when the poor dog was whining and licking the dead man's face—

most likely our dog was trying to be of help to the dead men. Dogs do that licking thing, and Latimer knew it. Spensor, as I said, was beyond a human being—the more bloody it was, the more he loved it."

"Well, he's having to answer to a higher authority now."

"Yes, sir. I heard he expired from the gunshot wound."

"Now Stockdale, where is Mr. Latimer? We lost him on the moor. Where would he go? We know he was hurt. We found bloodstains where he was last seen."

"London, I would suppose. He had a flat there somewhere. But he never confided in me."

"I see. You of course know this is just an initial statement and there will more detailed forthcoming interrogations?"

"Yes, sir."

"And once again you have been informed of your rights and this statement was not made under duress?"

"Yes, sir."

"And you had a court-appointed attorney here during these interviews."

"Yes, sir."

"That's all. Take him away.""

# Chapter 19

"Doc, I was flabbergasted when I heard it. The guys were after oil. They murdered for crude. The idea of oil was nowhere in my mind during this whole affair. I was used to New York street murder and drugs, Doc—nothing like oil ever crossed my blurred mind. The triangle of the homes that I plotted on the map was really a circle—an oil dome circle.

"Anyway, the hospital released me, and I found myself packing at the Princetown Hotel. I called the college and told them I was on the way back. Also, I knew that in the deep recesses of my mind that the nightmare would return when the hearings and trial began. I was still screwed up, Doc. I found myself crying in my room. I kept looking at my bandaged hand and then I'd see those eyes, those damn eyes. They would never leave me alone. Like farmer Hudson read in the Baskerville legend, we were 'ruined.' The words in the book kept coming back about how all those who had ever seen the hound were never the same. Never!

"I went down for dinner that evening, and Sergeant Hopkins was at the bar waiting for me.

*"Mind if I join you, Bill?"*

*"Of course not, Stanley."*

"We found a quiet table in the corner of the dining room.

*"I'm on extended leave with this arm. Seems they may need to operate on it again. I guess the only good thing is that I'm out of Dartmoor. Thank God."*

*"You are lucky."*

"The waiter came over and I ordered, but the sergeant just kept his drink.

*"The inspector is going nuts trying to find Latimer. All the districts and London are searching for him. He'll have to show up sometime. But to be honest, I think the bog might have got him and he's just been sucked away."*

*"Yes, maybe so. But I have an old cop feeling that the inspector has asked you to socialize with me to see if I can remember anything further about when he got away. Am I right, son?"*

*"Yes, sir. I'll not lie to you."*

*"Well, I know nothing more than I told him at the hospital. After I passed out from running and came to, he was gone."*

*"But, if you don't mind me asking, there seemed to be so much blood? Can Latimer's fall and tripping have banged him up that much that he lost so much blood? And if he lost so much blood, how could he then get back up and start running again? For that matter, you even had his blood on your face and clothes. And what about your burned hand? The inspector thinks you burned it when you jumped out of Hudson's lorry and maybe hit the hot tailpipe. But there are just too many things that don't fit. How does all this come into play, Bill?"*

*"I wish to God I knew, Stanley. Were there any prints found?"*

*"Hell, yes. Those damn big dog prints. They were all over the place. If you ask that, then you must have seen something, eh Bill? Was there a dog at the rocks?"*

"I couldn't answer, Doc. I just stared out the window. It was sunset and the moor was in tones of orange, rust colors, and gold. When I looked back, he was gone. I think he knew I was sick. Then when I saw the kitchen door open, the little girl was just looking at me. Doc, she came over to me still holding that small doll. She touched my bandaged hand.

> *"I have a mark too, my sweetheart. This old man, like you, has a burn on his hand."*

"She just turned away, Doc, and went back through the door. You know what? I never saw her again, but she has a place in my heart that is forever. Come to think about it, I think I have a place in her heart too.

"That night I had to drink myself to sleep. I killed a whole bottle. I remember I almost lost control from the depression. I had seen and been touched by something that no human is supposed to believe in. It was a fairy tale fiend. The hospital had declared me fit enough to be released, but I knew I was somehow going to have a complete breakdown. Before I passed out I had the shakes so bad, Doc, that I had to run to the toilet and I felt like my entire stomach was coming up."

"It's normal when such catastrophic events occur to a person. The body is trying to adjust to the trauma."

"Well, my body didn't do a very good job.

"The next day I was waiting for a cab to take me to Exeter. I wanted to be back at Cambridge so desperately. It was probably the prettiest day ever on the moor since I had been there. As I remember the colors were so strong. The thin air and wispy breeze was soft and even smelled so wonderfully earthen. I went over and looked across a vast reach of the hills and various size tors. I thought of Jenny, Doc. All the hell, the horror, the killing, and there I stood thinking of her. She was the only good thing I found on the moor, and I even lost that too. Perhaps I was a stranger who was not allowed there—at least I tried to reason like that. And when I invaded the landscape, it rebelled against me and punished me. I was looking desperately for answers you see, Doc. I just wanted some peace. I actually got on my knees in the room and pleaded to God for help. Hell, I hadn't prayed like that since I was an altar boy. I was so alone and I needed Him to do something for me. I needed to believe in Him."

"Yes, I see where you're coming from, Bill."

"When the cab arrived I looked straight ahead during the whole trip down the road. I never wanted to return there, Doc, never. I was 'ruined,' just as the legend had promised."

"Nonsense, Bill. We'll have you back to your old self in no time. So you went back to Cambridge?"

"Yes, but I didn't make it. What I mean is that I didn't do very well at class."

"How so?"

"Hell, they knew I was off my rocker. The first week, as I was giving a talk, suddenly I projected myself back on the moor. The next thing I knew they were leading me back to my room. They said I just went blank and stood there as if in a trance. The following week I went into another numb silence during a lecture—it happened just when I was talking about Holmes and the damn Baskerville story. They knew I wasn't gonna make it, Doc, so they bought me plane tickets and sent me back home."

"That was the right thing to do, Bill. Go on."

"I guess I was like a zombie, for months on end. I was living on pills and liquor. I seemed to sleep in the day and be awake all night. Everything was topsy-turvy. Then a letter came offering an all-expense-paid trip to the trial for Barney Stockdale. My mind went back to everything bad. I mean, I was so despondent. I didn't want to ever go back, Doc."

"So does this bring us up to where we are now, Bill?"

"No, not quite. I received this letter about two weeks ago. I thought I was actually doing better, Doc, until this came. That's when Father Flariety suggested I see you."

"So it has been months since you got back to the States?"

"Yes."

"You should have come sooner you know."

"Yeah, I know. But I had this thing about being a tough cop. That I could handle it and all that crap. Little did I know I was close to doing something dangerous."

"You mean you wanted to end it all?"

"Yes."

"Well, I think you have taken the first step to recovery, so we'll go through this together in order to make sense of all this turmoil."

"I think it's going to take more than that, Doc. When I got this letter I went bananas. That's when I was so desperate that Father Flariety knew I was near my end."

"Can I see it?"

"Sure. Here, I brought it with the tape."

"Better yet, you read it, Bill. I want to hear as you read it. In other words, I want to see your reaction."

"I don't think I'll make it through it, Doc. It gives me the shakes so damn bad."

"Just give it a try. If it doesn't work, then I'll read it."

"I may start this crying stuff again. I become nothing but a blubbering baby nowadays. I'm no longer a man, you see. I think I'm a juvenile. It takes nothing to start me crying."

"That's just part of your depression and the feeling of lonely helplessness coupled with your anxiety. Your mind and body are no longer in sync. But we'll bring you back around. So read the letter."

"Okay. Where are my glasses? Okay, here we go then.

*To: Mr. William Hughes*
*From: Sergeant Stanley Hopkins*
*Station Headquarters*
*Exeter, England*

186

*Dear Mr. Hughes,*

*I am writing this letter to thank you for all the assistance that you gave me when you were here. I know it's long overdue, but with trying to wrap up the case and attempting to locate Professor Harold Latimer, the Chief Inspector has about driven the chaps here at the department crazy. He retired about a month ago. He was a bit upset that he had to leave the force without finding Latimer. I think he was rather depressed about it when I saw him a few weeks ago at market. But now the news that I'm about to relate has lifted his spirits. Thanks to your efforts, I am up for promotion as they have noted I also helped break up the murder case. Of course the Chief Inspector and I knew it could have never come off without your discovery about the archeologist plot.*

*Furthermore, I wanted to let you know that the case is now officially closed as of two days ago. But for me, now there seems to be more unanswered questions, which I can honestly say border on the ridiculous. I'll try to give the details as they unfolded.*

*Two hikers were deep into the moor area, about where Abbot's Way path is located, but even farther away than the old path. They were in a barren part of the moor— some of the locals call it the wild area. No one really goes there much as you can imagine as it's just too far from anything. A sudden downpour came upon them and they ran for a small clump of boulders and found a natural cave caused by the leaning rocks. As they entered the cave, the couple noticed a shoe and a little farther back, another shoe. They went deeper inside and called to see if anyone else was in the chamber. Using their pack lights the male subject got to a point that a putrid smell was noticeable. The female companion retreated back to the entrance. Going farther inside, the male hiker flashed his torch and saw what were soiled clothes with bone and skin fragments protruding from pant legs and shirt sleeves. He also observed a half-fleshed skull separated from what was left of a torso.*

*Upon arriving at the scene, we discovered not one, but two dismembered bodies. The forensic lab said that the bodies were evidently partially consumed by an animal or animals. They further described canine tear and chew mark indications on both the flesh and bone fragments. Now get this, Mr. Hughes: identification found on one of the victim's clothing showed it to be Professor Latimer. So we believe this has brought this case to a close except for the trial of Mr. Stockdale. The other subject that was found farther inside the cave had evidently been there longer due to the deterioration of the corpse. He also had identification on his torn clothing, as one Wilfred Cabell."*

"Cabell? Is that the guy you first met at out on the moor?"

"Yeah, Doc, that's him."

"Go on. I didn't mean to interrupt."

"Okay, let's see where I was...

*Mr. Cabell had been missing for a while according to his family and was last known to have been in the Dartmoor area on a genealogical search. I checked on him and found out through a background check that he was recently released from prison on a fraud conviction. He evidently bilked hundreds of elderly people out of their savings on promises of some care health plan. He made millions. Of course these kind of criminal chaps, after hiring expensive barristers, get a slap on the wrist from the courts and then still come out wealthy from their ill-gotten gains. He evidently caused a lot of problems for many of the older people who were retired. A newspaper reported that it brought on a rash of desperate suicides among those he took advantage of during his fraud game.*

*We were at first confused as to why the subjects were so badly mauled and placed in the cave. But finally we have come to the only possible conclusion—that the two men were separately attacked by an animal pack while on the moors. We knew, of course, that Latimer was on the run, but are not sure of Cabell's circumstances.*

*Well, Bill, that's all I have on the case. Please let me know when you plan to arrive for Stockdale's trial. I'll pick you up at the airport. The court proceedings will be in London. Due to the notoriety of Mr. Stockdale, his attorneys had the proceedings moved out of Devon. Stay in touch.*

*Your friend,*
*Stanley"*

# Chapter 20

"Now, Doc, can I ask you a question?"

"Sure."

"Can I make it through the trial? Here I am, a nervous wreck about a courtroom, when sitting on a witness chair was second nature not two years ago."

"Of course, you'll do fine. Now is that about all, Bill?"

"Yeah, I think so."

"We'll have time to get you right prior to the trial. No problem. You'll see. Now what I'm about to tell you is just a quick synopsis here. We'll get into more detail later. Now don't argue back. I heard you out, now you hear me. Fair enough?"

"Fair enough, Doc. I'm all ears."

"Sometimes the mind can make us believe that we have heard and seen things that are as real as if you and I are sitting here across from each other. The mind can make thought patterns a reality for a person. The scenes and voices within the brain are so very real to that person. There is no way that this individual can be persuaded that these images and voices are not real, whether present or past experiences. They are imprinted into the psyche unless they are shown to be what they are, accidents in the memory. Once the accident is cleared up off the road, the path is straight again. The mind is free and clear of any of debris caused by that accident.

"So here we go on just a first impression. We'll counter each other as the session goes on. But once again, this is just a rough preliminary first thought that I feel may have happened, Bill.

"I think, first, that at your age, the ingestion of alcohol laced with a huge dose of LSD brought on illusions that night with your partner Clayton. Yes, you both saw a wild dog, wolf, moor pony, or whatever. But because of your conditions, you both had such a trip—or out-of-body LSD experience, so to speak—with such a cocktail combination that you still have those memories to this day. And, I'll be honest on this, you may have a bit of permanent damage. Evidently the amount of the hallucinogenic was such in that bottle that you completely went out of your mind. And that fellow Clayton evidently drank more than you did. That's why he has never come back. Bill, in blunt words, it toasted your brain. But I want you to know that you are treatable, even if there may be some damage. It will just take time and medication.

"Oh, I know what you want to say. 'What about the farmer? He saw it too.' You said yourself he was a drinker and on Wednesday evenings he loved to go to the pub at the inn. Surely there were times when he drank more than others. Maybe that night he tied one on...and maybe just after hearing at the bar about your experience, the episode festered in him. He had been hearing those sounds, and when he went to investigate, he could have been just plain drunk and scared already. He could have seen a shadow, or his own flashlight could have reflected on a wet rock and become glaring eyes, and that could have triggered him. Again, people are geared to folk and superstition. Just as the English police officer told you, as well as that professor, Latimer, Dartmoor is on the top of the pile for ghostly illusions and stories.

"As for the little girl, you wanted her to have seen the dog. She was afflicted, and yes she had a burn mark—but in your mentally roasted capacity, you wanted her to have encountered the hound. She never said she saw it; you told her she saw it. Anyway, she was just a child. And lastly, when you chased that Latimer guy on that evening, the whole first hallucinatory occurrence came back to your subconscious. Yes, he had tripped, hurt himself, and was bleeding badly, but that whole encounter with blood, the rocks, the mist, and the night made a throwback to the dog in your mental picture. As to animal prints on the ground, if Latimer was injured and bleeding, surely later in the night various predators would pick up the blood scent and come searching the scene. Thus the animal footprints. Wild carnivore moor animals are the only plausible reason for the bodies found in the cave by the hikers.

"Now about the scar on your hand. That is a puzzle to me. Maybe you did scorch it on the muffler pipe as the inspector indicated, but in your memory you made it identify with the events as you perceived them and also with that little girl. You burned yourself somehow, and when we go further into this we'll discover how that wound happened. You see, the mind is still uncharted, and of course there are many things beyond our understanding at this time. If you can look at the basic..."

He went on and on with his first analysis. Bill listened but could not believe. He kept silent but his mind responded, *Was I in Never-Never Land? Maybe I am off my rocker, but you can never make me admit I didn't see that pitch-black monster.*

"Now, it has been a hell of a long day—good heavens, Bill, it's six-thirty! Still, I want you to sum up your feelings, like this is a last chapter in a book, so to speak."

Bill put his head back on the thick chair and stared at the ceiling. He thought about a cigarette, then let it pass. He waited until he could get his thoughts into some kind of organized pattern, then he began. Dr. Hansom didn't rush him but just waited for him to start.

"Doc, I heard what you just said, and perhaps you're onto something, but in my heart, after all this, I believe evil begets evil. After all these months, and now in talking to you, I somehow feel that maybe this thing, this creature or beast, only destroyed evil. It was itself an evil demon for sure, but maybe it hunted and measured out a hellish justice on corrupt people. I don't know exactly what I'm trying to say, but I wonder if we who accidentally came in contact with the black dog were just in the wrong place at the wrong time. It never killed those who somehow were not deemed ultimately evil. We were just haphazardly in the way when we came upon the hound. It never attacked the child, me, Clayton, or Mr. Morse Hudson. Oh, it scared the living shit out of us, but it never destroyed us physically— mentally yes, as it was said before, it 'ruined' one. Its lick was maybe some type of gesture as any dog would do, but unknowingly it caused pain, and it left its mark or brand not only on the skin but in the brain and soul.

"As for Jenny, and this sounds corny, but I see her standing on a rock ledge overlooking the moor. The wind is rippling her divine red hair and next to her is the hound. But he's gentle and she has her hand around his neck. He growls, but only this time it's not menacing. That's how I see things, Doc. Hell, I'm not sure what the crap I'm even talking about, I'm just so tired now. But I feel all this inside me."

Both were quiet for the next few minutes as if digesting what each other had said.

"You're right, Bill—your ending does sound like a Hollywood movie. You must understand that we must face the actual reality of all this as we progress in the sessions. I want you to take these pills twice a day with a lot of fluids—and I don't mean alcohol. No heavy cocktailing until I tell you. It's no longer a choice. A beer is okay and a glass of wine, but no more hard stuff. Is that understood?"

"Yeah."

"I'll be out of these offices next week, so here is my phone number. And the following week we can take up where we left off at my apartment. As for the coming trial and reliving all this again, give it your best effort, try not to worry, and just be strong, Bill. You're a rough ex-cop, just be tough a little longer. You've got to hold on. As I said, we'll have you fit as a fiddle in the very near future. I expect you to feel an improvement after about four visits. Then after more visits, God willing, you'll be your old self again. As a matter of fact, just this spilling of your deep-seated memories will let you have a better sleep tonight. You'll see. You'll get a good night's rest tonight."

Bill left the office and walked out to the night world of horns, screeching tires, street sounds, and flashing lights. There was no doubt in his mind he would have to go back to the psychiatrist's office—he was all he had to depend on. It was either him or no rational sanity at all. As he walked toward the subway, the red brake lights of snarled traffic still sent some type of emotional upheaval to his stomach. Then he uncontrollably whispered a prayer.

"Father Flariety, for God's sake, pray for me."

# Chapter 21

Early November 1982. 525 East 86$^{th}$ Street, New York City. Bill's knock was answered by Dr. Hansom and he entered the apartment. All Bill's previous sessions had been in the psychiatrist's office, which never seemed to be able to close due to delays in cleaning out the furniture. The doctor's flat was extremely different than his place of work had been. While Dr. Hansom's office was sedate and warm with reddish-toned leather chairs plus expensive oriental rugs, the apartment was the modern style of hard-edged chrome along with a black-and-white color scheme for the fabrics accented by stark chalk-white walls. The floors were laid pine planks with ceiling spotlights flooding the various modern paintings.

Dr. Hansom quickly gave Bill an outward diagnosis. Bill had gained some weight and looked better than he had when he had first started the visits. His demeanor and dress were much improved as well. But the patient's eyes said there was still an uneasiness lurking inside and that uneasiness stared hard into the doctor's pupils. For a silent moment they both tried to adjust to the reunion.

"Well hello, Bill," the doctor began. "It's good to see you again."

"You too, Doc." Bill took in the surroundings. "Your home is certainly different than the office."

"Oh yes, my wife and my daughter are decorators and I have always liked the difference of settings. I found the change refreshing after a day of four walls in the office."

"The art is really striking, Doc. I like it a lot."

"Yes, I thought you might. We do also—it's fresh and alive...sort of in tune with our lifestyle. Now with my retirement I plan to see many galleries. My wife has our itinerary for a trip to France soon."

A large painting greeted Bill as he emerged into the living room.

"That's not an original Warhol piece is it?"

"Yep. One of his early tomato can efforts, and over the piano is a Lichtenstein.

"Ah, the cartoon man.

"You amaze me, Bill. You are, as they say, a learned man!"

"I try, Doc."

"Look in the dining room, Bill. That's a Jasper Johns."

Bill saw a large fabric American flag crinkled and stretched across a canvas. It had a glued-on appearance and seemed as if it could peel off at any moment.

"Come on in my study, Bill."

Even Dr. Hansom's hideaway was eclectic. The walls and ceiling were painted a shiny enamel black, and the bookshelves, which were stuffed with books, were stainless steel. Various sized statues from religious cults were strategically placed on pedestals and inside the library shelves. Sitting on four stone columns was a massive, irregularly shaped piece of black granite with small streaks of a copper effervescent. This impressive object was used as a desk, and Bill was hit with an appreciation of what many bucks could obtain. Office files were still in cardboard boxes close to the oversized, leather desk chair. Large bamboo lounge chairs with checkered black and off-white fabric coordinated wonderfully with the zebra rug laid out on the floor. On the wall behind the desk was a mix of prints and small paintings.

"These works are mostly of the Ash-Can period. Are you familiar with those guys?"

"A little. They were the gritty artists weren't they? They liked the slums, alleys, boxing rings, and my cop side of the world."

"Excellent, Bill. You got it."

"I bet those pieces set you back plenty."

"I must admit I overindulge, but that's my hobby. I don't play golf or pay enormous dollars for sports events and other attractions. Of course I do like studying religions, as I previously mentioned to you, plus classical music and opera as you also do. But let's get down to the matter at hand shall we? Sit there and we'll start. I'm anxious to know what has transpired while you were gone."

"Sure, Doc."

"Why don't you start with your last appointment? What happened after that?"

"Well, Doc, after my third visit to your office and popping the various prescriptions you gave me, I was feeling rested and somewhat whole again. Oh, I'll be honest, there were a few waking night sweats and may be a yelp or two when I would abruptly awaken from a disturbed dream, but I was in better control and the despondent bouts had all but ceased. Thanks to you I was feeling a bit more like my old self, at least physically.

"Then the call came. The airline tickets with accommodation confirmations in London followed by mail, arriving in a Scotland Yard envelope. The court date was for the second week in September. For some reason I felt I was ready for the trial of Barney Stockdale, as ready as I could ever be to feel the sting of the defense lawyers while in the witness chair.

"Sergeant Stanley Hopkins kept his word and was there when I entered Heathrow air terminal. He looked good and as we drove to the hotel, he went on about the various operations he had had on his wounded elbow. But the best news was that Stanley's promotion had been approved and he was expecting it to come through any day. His upbeat attitude affected me, and somehow we ended up laughing about all the hell we went through. He told me the good news that the two farmers' wives had sold their farms and had gone to join their children. The bad news was that Constable Clayton had not improved at all.

"At the hotel bar, Hopkins revealed what had happened since the letter he sent me.

*"I need to bring you up-to-date, Bill, as to what's happened in the last few months. We looked around the colleges who had geology curriculums and eventually found that Latimer had attended Camborne School of Mines. Through that process we found where he had lived and discovered he had a brother residing in the town of Tipton. Latimer's brother told us that their father was an engineer and involved with the discovery of the Sherwood Forest oil field. That oil find was top secret at the time because of the German bombing raids. During the war period, crude was more valuable than gold, you see."*

*"No doubt."*

*"Later, after the war, Latimer's dad roamed around Dartmoor and took the boys on his excursions. He surmised that there was a dome—perhaps the largest dome of oil in England—sitting just under the Dartmoor hills. After finishing school at Camborne, Latimer worked in Arabia, Libya, and the North Atlantic oil regions. Upon arriving back home many years later, his brother said he confessed secretly that he had been involved in a killing in Arabia. Latimer's brother noted that he had become different, distant, and not the man he once knew. To him, Latimer seemed like he had a mental problem and he was always nervous. Then came his obsession with his father's Dartmoor idea and he all but disappeared from the family in*

Tipton. *So far that's all we got, but we're still digging."*

*"Oil...of all things, oil."*

*"Yeah. On top of that, we contacted other geologists on the idea and they all but laughed at us when we brought the crude prospect up. They said the strata is not there for oil."*

"The next day I was introduced to the Crown's prosecuting attorneys. They were nice enough—perhaps stuffy—but they made me feel somewhat inferior. Over and over they rehearsed me on what to expect and how to put on the act for their brand of courtroom procedure.

*"Be positive and assured on your answers, Mr. Hughes!"*

"What the hell, did they think I was an amateur in courtroom theatrics?"

"Your feelings are understandable. Go on, Bill."

"Well, none of their coaching mattered in the end, Doc, because I never made it to the witness chair. On the second day of the trial, Mr. Stockdale changed his innocent plea to guilty. He received forty-five years. But as paroles go, he will be out in less time.

"I was free again to go home. I felt almost jubilant at being spared the questioning of what had happened on the moor, but a whisper of anxiety made me still nervous of the days to come. I knew I was not quite there yet—my peace of mind was still entangled in the Dartmoor mists. Doc, I know your viewpoint on my experience and what caused my memories, and had the trial continued, I have no doubt the defense attorney would have insisted my memory was tainted by the LSD, just as you do. But to tell you the truth, I still believe my version of what happened on the moor. It's like it has become anchored in the deepest part of my psyche.

"Anyway, as I walked from the hall of justice and down the

busy streets of London, my total mindset was on the uncanny luck of getting my flight to New York rescheduled for the next morning, thanks to Sergeant Hopkins. After about a fifteen minute walk, I turned the corner and went into a small lunch cafe sort of place. It was not a block from my hotel, and being after the noon hour, there were very few patrons. I sat down at an empty table. As I browsed the small table menu, a soft voice came from my side.

*"May I take your order, sir?"*

"When I looked up, it was like a thunderbolt hit me!

*"Jenny!""*

# Chapter 22

"You mean it was the reverend's wife, Jenny?"

"None other, Doc. I couldn't believe it. All those days and nights of wondering about her. As you know, she had never really left me, even though she had walked out of my life into the moor mist months earlier. We talked briefly then and I could tell she was pleased to see me. We arranged that I would meet her there when her shift ended. As I walked away from the café, I was ecstatic. It seemed too good to be true.

"I was waiting for her early that evening when she got off work. We found a pub nearby and settled into a quiet table. It was like we picked up where we'd left off on the moor. She needed someone to confide in, and for whatever reason, she felt safe with me. She told me she had been hiding away from her husband and the world. She went on to say her existence was meager but so free—free as the Dartmoor ponies on the moor. But she went on to say that her guilt of leaving her husband continually pressed on her every day, Doc."

"Yes, I could see that. Go on."

"Jenny confessed that she had previously written her parents that she was planning to leave her husband in a way that would not be disgraceful to him in regard to a divorce. It amazed me that her parents complied, and then I realized why they were so quiet when they arrived at the hotel in Dartmoor. They knew she had planned her disappearance.

"Jenny told me a lot more about her life, and I really came to understand her. The physical urge for her changed—I wanted to know her heart and mind. I know you don't want to hear her whole life story, so I'll try to summarize the main points."

"That's good, Bill."

"She explained that when she became a minister's wife, she was plunged into a world of overwhelming public exhibition. The open-door policy to their home began immediately after the marriage vows were said, and as the congregation flooded in, their time together grew less and less. Even the standard fifteen months of newlywed bliss was denied them. As her husband drifted more into caring for his flock—and into impressing the higher-ups—her life seemed to continually take second place. Jenny found herself pushed into personal isolation. Their dinner conversation was always about the various parishioner problems or the Bishop's latest request, never about their cares or feelings for one another. But Carl had warned her about the sacrifice of losing her personal life if she married him and she had agreed, so she felt she needed to stifle her complaints and just cope with it. And when she did try to talk with him about their relationship, he just told her to try harder.

"Jenny told me that she had loved the church as a child, especially when they would attend a service at one of the great cathedrals. Even when she was too young to understand the messages, she loved the music, the grand ecclesiastical architecture, the sense of awe and reverence. She met Carl when she was in her early twenties and was impressed by his devotion to his work. His 'calling' seemed so noble to her at the time. But she had long since realized that her more mystical form of faith did not fit in the hierarchical world of church politics.

"The narrow village social scene that was so important to the church women also failed to satisfy Jenny's more artistic imagination. Instead of growing into caring for her husband's church, Jenny felt alienated as her attempts of communicating never seemed to measure up, especially with the ladies and the various clubs and organizations within the church and village. She was out of her sphere. The months and years grew more desolate as her husband badgered her to become more than she was capable of being. He was never content with her attempts at organizing church socials and children's programs. The holidays were excruciating as she had to pretend happiness in front of her husband's friends and superiors. She eventually felt herself sliding into the shadows and all but gave up hope of any success as a pastor's wife.

"Jenny struggled along like this for several years. The collapse of her marriage really began when a new doctor moved into the small town. His name was James LePrince, married with two children, and he joined the ranks of Reverend Williamson's church. At first it was the casual glances, she said, but the true moment happened at a church flea market. She and Jim, as she called him, were thrown together working a fortune-telling booth, he as the genie and she as the gypsy. In order to show him how the cards worked, she demonstrated by telling her own fortune. She spread the cards out in front of him and read them. The cards foretold that she was to meet a new male friend that day who would affect her everyday life. She told me they laughed at the possibility of a preacher's wife having an affair, but the chuckle ended as they found themselves connecting—connecting in emotions and denied feelings, connecting in a desperate grasp of wanting to feel the romance that had been so long absent.

"I remember her eyes glistening wet, Doc, when she said those things weren't supposed to happen in God's protected house. But within three months they consummated the relationship under a massive, shaded oak tree. That was the one moment when she became distant from me, Doc. She talked about the oak tree and how it sat on a hill overlooking a windswept and waving wheat field. It was like she was returning there even while I was sitting across from her and loving her.

"We talked for hours, and I could tell that sharing with me had been cathartic for her. When I got back to my hotel that night, I changed my plans. I had expected the trial to last longer, so my schedule was completely clear. I found a cheaper hotel, since I was no longer on the Crown's dime—or should I say pence? I stayed in London and Jenny let me enter her life.

"A few days later she finally told me the rest of the story of LePrince. Seems they lived the life of tortured secrecy, which unnerved both of them, plus they feared the consequences of being discovered. But unlike a purely emotional love affair, theirs had crossed over to a parish sacrilege. She said she anguished over how much longer the infidelity could continue until they were found out. They both knew the moment of decision was coming. He wanted it to end and told her; then she also knew that things would come crashing down. Both were desperate to tell their spouses for some kind of release. But to no avail—they still found themselves under the oak tree.

"It was on April 23, 1980, that the world collapsed for Jenny. I recollect that date, Doc, for some reason."

"Yeah, certain cycles and events do have a way of impressing on the brain, Bill. Go on."

"Let's see…where was I?"

"You had mentioned a date."

"Yeah, yeah, the date."

"You see, Dr. James LePrince's car hit a country tractor, which was instantly fatal. Not only did Jenny have her own shock and grief to deal with, but as the minister's wife, she was expected to comfort the grieving widow. All this time she was uncertain whether the affair had been discovered. Not long before the accident, Jenny felt something was different about her husband. He had begun to retreat and become quiet. Did he know? But how could he? She and

Jim had been so careful. Was it the syndrome of husband-and-wife instinct that no closed door could hide? As she plodded along in a state of numbness through the week of the funeral, she couldn't tell if her secret was known but being covered up to preserve respectability, or if they had not yet been discovered.

"Somehow Jenny continued to do her duties despite the passion being gone from her life, and things continued this way for more than a year. Then what she had feared came to pass. Mrs. LePrince sold her house and was disposing of her husband's papers in preparation for the move. She found a letter he had composed to Jenny just days before his death attempting once more to break off their forbidden love affair. It had never been sent. She shared it with one of the elders' wives, who told Carl. Jenny told me she felt like the few remaining bits of her privacy dissolved into oblivion. All was out in the open as the church gossips spread the news. But Jim was gone and no one wanted to attack the memory of the man who had been eulogized as a great village doctor and father. So Jenny was left alone to reap the blame and disgust of being a parson's unfaithful wife.

"Doc, Jenny told me that she secretly longed to just disappear. She longed to be able to make a fresh start somewhere brand new—where no one knew her mistakes, where no one had any expectations of her. Another doctor's learned advice to her husband was to place her in a rest home atmosphere, and the church bulletin announced that Jenny 'was convalescing due to overwork and exhaustion.' But the rectory door had already been opened for all the assembly to peer in. Rector Carl Williamson found himself removed and relegated to a small working man's community. Jenny said she could never forget her husband breaking down in front of her when he got the news, which compounded the whole lurid mess. That was the state of affairs when I first met them in Dartmoor."

"Let's take a break here. As a matter of fact, let's call it a day."

"Good, Doc, I'm sorta tired at that."

"Won't you come around...say...about ten tomorrow? We can then try to finish up."

"Okay, Doc. Ten o'clock it is. Can I say something?"

"Of course."

"Like I said, I'm exhausted. But you know, Doc, I feel easy. I mean, I'm drained but sorta flushed out. I—"

"No need to go on, Bill. I understand. Take these tablets for this evening."

As the patient closed the door, Dr. Hansom looked at the clock.

"God, I'm late again. Sarah is going to kill me! I'll never make it to the restaurant."

# Chapter 23

Bill returned the next day and settled in the doctor's study.

"So Bill, you told me a lot about Jenny's story yesterday. I'd like to know more about how meeting her again affected you, and how that relates to your experiences in Dartmoor."

"Okay, Doc. Well, like I said, I was overjoyed that Jenny was willing to confide in me. You know I had longed to be part of her life, had wanted her to need me somehow. I felt like during those days in London I became her medicine. She had given herself freedom by disappearing that day in Dartmoor, but when I came back into her life, I believe she began looking at her past again, not just running from it. I found myself listening, reasoning, supporting, and even caressing her during her self-guilt crying bouts.

"And then I found myself confiding to Jenny about the Dartmoor nightmare. I was embarrassed at first because I started shaking whenever I spoke of the unnatural events. But she had poured out her heart to me, so it seemed to be a sort of way of reciprocating. I no longer just wanted her physically, Doc, although I certainly still did that. I found myself needing her to comfort me too. I won't repeat what I said to her, Doc, as you already know the story, but she was a good listener. She had been there, Doc. She had seen that creature from afar, and somehow I knew that she didn't think I was completely crazy."

Bill paused as if deciding whether to say the next part.

"Doc, can I tell you what happened when we first came together?"

"Sure…it helps to know emotions."

"I had felt like I was going to be her hero when I met her in Dartmoor. Somehow I had convinced myself I would be able sweep her away from Carl if only I had the chance. But Carl was in the way, Doc. I wanted *him* out of the way and instead *she* disappeared. My idea of heroics was just self-indulging…a man's thing of bravado. I pretended she needed me. In reality, all along we were both grasping to have something to hold on to and not be alone. To be honest, we began our nights together by clinging together for support and protection.

"When we first embraced a few weeks after we met in London, we both knew our feelings without words. We just stood there and held each other. No words Doc, just squeezing each other till we could hardly breathe. I had visions while I was at Dartmoor of a fiercely passionate sexual encounter between us, but when we arrived home from dinner one night to her flat we dissolved into almost a slow-motion, soft coming together. When we touched each other for the first time, I no longer wanted to go to heaven…she was heaven. I could not stop saying over and over that I loved her, and I barely let her take a breath without my lips on hers. Doc, at the end I swear we merged. Can it be that way, Doc? I mean can two people really dissolve into each other? Can one part live without the other?"

"What happened later, Bill? How were your emotions in the following days?"

"Well, Doc, I continued to love her and need her as much as ever, but I was still inwardly scared. Time tends to somewhat heal pain, but the mind tattoos memories and I reasoned Jenny and I both needed more time."

"Is that when you returned to New York?"

"No, not yet. On a raw October morning Jenny called me at my thrifty hotel. She was having trouble even speaking so I couldn't tell what was wrong. I rushed over to her flat. Jenny, in her robe, was sitting at her breakfast table. Her eyes were closed tight, but the water still leaked out. I picked up the folded newspaper that lay under her fingers—it was the religious section. It said that Reverend Carl Williamson, on Sunday last, had suffered a fatal stroke while in his pulpit in the village of Crofty, in West Glamorgan.

"She said she killed him, Doc. Jenny said that her selfish actions killed her husband as sure as if she had murdered him.

*"I killed him, Bill. I stabbed him in his heart. It was no stroke...I killed him. I turned his ministry into hell. And all his praying...I washed away all his hopes."*

*"You are to never think like that, Jenny. Never! You are who you are and he was who he was...two very different people. Your world was music, the arts, privacy, and enjoying the side of life that only you knew best. His was community, Jenny, his was serving others and wanting you to follow his ideals. He put your hopes on the shelf. You said there was never any time for you both to be lovers...never any time for the peace that the church preaches about over and over. You were coming to a crisis and you reached out for love. That love ended up horribly, I grant you—you lost your desperate reach for love with the accident, and then you lost your husband's. Finally the congregation threw stones at you as the Bible relates. No, you had to leave, Jenny. You had to."*

*"But I remember Carl said if I married him we would end up in Canterbury. He said with me at his side all things would be possible. We would live in Camelot. Bill, I let him down...I can never excuse what I did to him. I..."*

"I let her be with herself the rest of the day. She needed inner healing and not more words."

"That's good, Bill. Sometimes time alone is the only thing a person can face."

"After that day apart, we clung onto each other like magnets. It was as if we needed each other to survive. You know, Doc, we had both been to hell and back. What else was left but…up. Eventually it was as if we had talked enough about the past, and we felt the mercy of just plain relief. We went out, saw shows, visited antique fairs, tried to poison each other with our cooking, and then the laughter of each other's mistakes took over. God, I loved her!

"Then I came back. I refused her offer to move into her apartment. Hell, we both thought we still needed time and were living in a fantasy. But those fantasy weeks seemed magical. I'd lived through an unspeakable nightmare, and then somehow something wonderful came out of it. But Jenny had worked so hard for her freedom, and there I was monopolizing her life. I was determined to give Jenny her space. She too said we needed time.

"But Jesus, I have screwed up so bad. Time and distance is a destroyer, Doc. I screwed up by coming back here…everything started downhill and now I'm right back where I was."

"Are you still in contact?"

"Well, yes, we've talked. But we're both scared again. She called me and said as much."

"I see."

It was over. Bill sat back and the psychiatrist arose and went over to the small refrigerator next to some bookshelves. He opened it, took out two chilled glasses, placed them on the desk, then brought out a tray of ice cubes from the small freezer. Uncaringly he tapped it on his desk releasing the ice crystals that tried to escape over the loose papers. He placed them in the glasses, opened a drawer, and out came a scotch bottle with an unfamiliar label. He poured each glass half full.

"Here, drink this. It's very old and expensive."

Bill sipped the elixir. It burned as he expected.

"Burns like a cheap Scotch to me, Doc."

"You are something else, Bill," Hansom rebuffed the remark.

The doctor eased himself into the desk chair. He swept most of the papers off to the side of the cluttered desk and began to write on a crumpled piece of paper.

"Drink it, Bill, damn it. Don't sip it, gulp it down."

"What about the doctor's code of ethics with the alcohol or whatever it's called?"

"I no longer need to have any code...remember I'm through. My turn to let loose."

"You can smoke if you want to, Bill."

Bill followed the doctor's drinking orders and lit a cigarette. Hansom fired up a large cigar. Then Hansom reinforced the drinks.

"See that filter on the wall?"

"Yeah."

"My wife put in a smoke filtering system. She hates cigars."

"I like cigars too."

"These are Cuban...the best. Want one?"

"I thought they were illegal to import?"

"They are. Want one? Much healthier than those things in your mouth."

"Okay...if the doctor prescribes it."

"I do. It sorta feels like absolution after a long discourse."

"Very funny, Doc."

As Dr. Hansom brought out another cigar from a dark mahogany humidor, he snipped off the end, gave it to his patient, lit it for him, and leaned back in his oversized leather chair.

"As you are my last case, I beg your indulgence. I deserve this numbness. I want to get smashed with you. I deserve it. But before we crash, I wanted to write you a prescription to take. You must get it filled as soon as possible."

Another round was poured, then another. They were starting

to snicker, coupled with quick remarks and short sharp laughs.

"God, my wife is going to murder me when she gets in. She despises me when I go over the top of the bottle...but what the hell...she's never been able to put up with me anyhow."

"You're a hell of a shrink, Doc."

Dr. Hansom answered Bill's compliment, "Yeah, not bad for a Jewish, Catholic, Pentecostal, Buddhist, Mormon, and whatever swami."

The alcohol flowed and so did the cutting jokes about one another.

"So this is how my practice ends......a dog bite." His summation was slurry. Then he laughed out loud.

"Wha'd'ya mean? All you do is sit on your ass and listen to other people's problems and rake in the cash all day!"

"Yeah, sorta like a cop sitting in a car or office, taking tidbits and rip-offs from gangs on the side." The doctor's words were subdued.

The alcohol was bringing on the inner honesty of feelings.

"Hell, I guess our professions are sorta alike. Only you rip off with a notepad and a lounge chair...and we get it off the streets."

"You can be an asshole, Bill..."

"So can you. You never even began to believe me. You think I'm too late for help. *Just get him out*, that's what you're thinking."

"Your anxiety level is growing, Bill. I never said that. Calm down."

Bill's voice took a leap in tone. "'Get healing advice,' said the priest. It's nothing but scotch and a prescription. To hell with you...you and Father Flariety. Just two false prophets."

"Down, Bill, easy. We should have not celebrated with this stuff. Bad advice from a retired doctor I guess."

"What's there to celebrate? Now I got this God damn dog burn mark on my hand and inside my head. Even worse, I'm scared of bringing Jenny into my screwed up life."

"Take this, you bastard, for your long-term treatment. Take this prescription and get out so I can try to get right before I have to meet my wife."

"What is it? Two dog biscuits and a glass of hot milk before bed?"

"Get your ass out of here and take this with you!"

The doctor half tossed the folded paper across the desk, but it missed Bill's fingers and glided to the floor.

Bill Hughes reached down, spilling some of his amber liquid on the paper and rug.

"You're spoiling my rug."

"What the hell do you care? You're unchained, you're free…no more loonies to put up with. My prescription, huh? My cure, huh? You're a failure, Doc. A failure! I trusted in you. You were my last hope."

Dr. Hansom leaned back on his chair, took a deep drag from his cigar, and eased the white cloud out of his mouth. "It was a mistake to celebrate with you. Maybe I am a failure, so please get out."

They were fed up with one another. Each hoped to end the words and separate.

"Screw you, Doc…you and that bent priest."

"Get out!"

Bill knew he was drunk as he punched the elevator buttons. First up then down. As he pushed on the apartment revolving door, he almost stumbled into the crowded sidewalk. He couldn't help noticing that people were avoiding him. *Drunk at two o'clock in the afternoon,* he thought. *What the hell happened?* he wondered, *everything was going so good only a few hours ago. It was the doctor's fault,* he reasoned, *he caused all this.*

He found refuge against a block wall in a small alley alcove.

He dug into his pocket and brought out the folded paper smelling of scotch aroma. It was liquor-stained and the ink was blurred, but it was readable.

"Jesus Christ!"

His wail brought quick attention from bypassing pedestrians, who gave him a quick glance into the alley, then no longer bothered to care.

The note read, "GO GET HER."

# The Finale

On June 18, 1983, on a miserable rainy day, Old St. Anne's Catholic Church in New York was the setting for Jenny Williamson and Bill Hughes to joyously exchange vows. Father Flariety served as the officiate. The bridesmaid was the elderly Sister Lilly, and the groomsman was Dr. E.P. Hansom. Invited guests on the groom's side of the pews were his apartment neighbors, including Rico, the guy who used to pound on his door at night and curse him. The apartment had finally found a little tranquility. Seated on the bride's side of the church were the six ladies who were always faithful at the Saturday afternoon confessions. The music played on the broken organ was of course off-key and unbelievably out of cadence, but the soloist did her best to fulfill Bill's request. It was one of Jenny's tunes that she had played when they first met at the inn, "You'll Never Walk Alone." Bill specifically asked the woman organist to please not sing, but when the priest told the groom that he could kiss the bride, out came the aged, squeaky falsetto rendition that bounced back and forth off the gothic stone walls.

*"When you walk through a storm,*
*hold your head up high and don't*
*be afraid of the dark.*
*At the end of the storm is a golden sky,*
*and the sweet silver song of the lark.*
*Walk on through the wind,*
*walk on through the rain,*

*Tho' your dreams be tossed and blown.*
*Walk on, walk on with hope in your heart*
*and you'll never walk alone,*
*you'll never, ever walk alone."*

Everything about the music was wrong, and Bill and Jenny were laughing to the point of tears as they touched lips.

----------- ----------- -----------

Three months later out on Dartmoor, a lone hiker watched the yellow disc of the evening sun merge into a kaleidoscope of colors as it neared the crest of a craggy outcrop of boulders. What heavenly peace. *Wait! What was that?* A noise barely absorbed itself into his ear. It was so distant that it mixed into the rush of the breeze combined with the whistling scrub grass, but it was there nonetheless. A whining, forlorn sound. It unnerved him at first, but his reasoning overcame his human suspicion of the unexplained. There it was again. It echoed in long, agonizing tremolo vibrations. *It must have been some sheep dog,* he thought.

Yes, that could be the only explanation.

FINIS

Also from MX Publishing

Close To Holmes

A Look at the Connections Between Historical London, Sherlock Holmes and Sir Arthur Conan Doyle.

Eliminate The Impossible

An Examination of the World of Sherlock Holmes on Page and Screen.

The Norwood Author

Arthur Conan Doyle and the Norwood Years (1891 - 1894) – Winner of the 2011 Howlett Literary Award (Sherlock Holmes book of the year)

Also From MX Publishing

In Search of Dr Watson

Wonderful biography of
Dr.Watson from expert Molly
Carr – 2$^{nd}$ edition fully updated.

Arthur Conan Doyle, Sherlock
Holmes and Devon

A Complete Tour Guide and
Companion.

The Lost Stories of Sherlock Holmes

Eight more stories from the pen of John
H Watson – compiled by Tony
Reynolds.

www.mxpublishing.com

# Also From MX Publishing

Watsons Afghan Adventure

Fascinating biography of Watson's time in Afghanistan from US Army veteran Kieran McMullen.

Shadowfall

Sherlock Holmes, ancient relics and demons and mystic characters. A supernatural Holmes pastiche.

Official Papers of The Hound of The Baskervilles

Very unusual collection of the original police papers from The Hound case.

Also From MX Publishing

The Sign of Fear

The first adventure of the 'female Sherlock Holmes'. A delightful fun adventure with your favourite supporting Holmes characters.

A Study in Crimson

The second adventure of the 'female Sherlock Holmes' with a host of sub-plots and new characters joining Watson and Fanshaw

The Chronology of Arthur Conan Doyle

The definitive chronology used by historians and libraries worldwide.

www.mxpublishing.com

Also From MX Publishing

Aside Arthur Conan Doyle

A collection of twenty stories from ACD's close friend Bertram Fletcher Robinson.

Bertram Fletcher Robinson

The comprehensive biography of the assistant plot producer of The Hound of The Baskervilles

Wheels of Anarchy

Reprint and introduction to Max Pemberton's thriller from 100 years ago. One of the first spy thrillers of its kind.

Also From MX Publishing

The Outstanding Mysteries of Sherlock Holmes

With thirteen Homes stories and illustrations Kelly re-creates the gas-lit, fog-enshrouded world of Victorian London

Rendezvous at The Populaire

Sherlock Holmes has retired, injured from an encounter with Moriarty. He's tempted out of retirement for an epic battle with the Phantom of the opera.

Baker Street Beat

An eclectic collection of articles, essays, radio plays and 'general scribblings' about Sherlock Holmes from Dr.Dan Andriacco.

www.mxpublishing.com

Also From MX Publishing

The Case of The Grave Accusation

The creator of Sherlock Holmes has been accused of murder. Only Holmes and Watson can stop the destruction of the Holmes legacy.

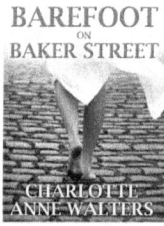

Barefoot on Baker Street

Epic novel of the life of a Victorian workhouse orphan featuring Sherlock Holmes and Moriarty.

Case of Witchcraft

A tale of witchcraft in the Northern Isles, in which long-concealed secrets are revealed -- including some that concern the Great Detective himself!

www.mxpublishing.com

# Also From MX Publishing

The Affair In Transylvania

Holmes and Watson tackle Dracula in deepest Transylvania in this stunning adaptation by film director Gerry O'Hara

The London of Sherlock Holmes

400 locations including GPS co-ordinates that enable Google Street view of the locations around London in all the Homes stories

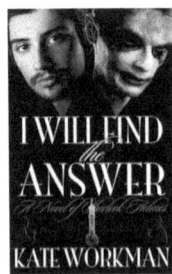

I Will Find The Answer

Sequel to Rendezvous At The Populaire, Holmes and Watson tackle Dr.Jekyll.

www.mxpublishing.com

Also From MX Publishing

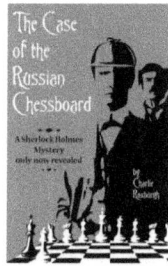

The Case of The Russian Chessboard

Short novel covering the dark world of
Russian espionage sees Holmes and
Watson on the world stage facing dark
and complex enemies.

An Entirely New Country

Covers Arthur Conan Doyle's years
at Undershaw where he wrote
Hound of The Baskervilles.
Foreword by Mark Gatiss (BBC's
Sherlock).

Shadowblood

Sequel to Shadowfall, Holmes and
Watson tackle blood magic, the vilest
form of sorcery.

www.mxpublishing.com

Also From MX Publishing

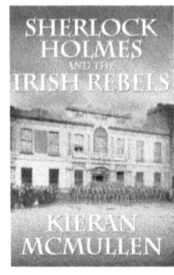

Sherlock Holmes and The Irish Rebels

It is early 1916 and the world is at war. Sherlock Holmes is well into his spy persona as Altamont.

The Punishment of Sherlock Holmes

*"deliberately and successfully funny"*

The Sherlock Holmes Society of London

No Police Like Holmes

It's a Sherlock Holmes symposium, and murder is involved. The first case for Sebastian McCabe.

www.mxpublishing.com

Also From MX Publishing

In The Night, In The Dark

Winner of the Dracula Society Award – a collection of supernatural ghost stories from the editor of the Sherlock Holmes Society of London journal.

Sherlock Holmes and The Lyme Regis Horror

Fully updated 2$^{nd}$ edition of this bestselling Holmes story set in Dorset.

My Dear Watson

Winner of the Suntory Mystery Award for fiction and translated from the original Japanese. Holmes greatest secret is revealed – Sherlock Holmes is a woman.

www.mxpublishing.com